D1432096

Mountains
Hidden in the

Fort Seybert 1758

ROBIN PROPST KILE

LifeRich
PUBLISHING

This is a work of fiction. All of the characters, names, incidents,
organizations, and dialogue in this novel are either the products
of the author's imagination or are used fictitiously.

LifeRich Publishing is a registered trademark of
The Reader's Digest Association, Inc.

LifeRich Publishing books may be ordered through booksellers or by contacting:

LifeRich Publishing
1663 Liberty Drive
Bloomington, IN 47403
www.liferichpublishing.com
1 (888) 238-8637

Because of the dynamic nature of the Internet, any web addresses or
links contained in this book may have changed since publication and
may no longer be valid. The views expressed in this work are solely those
of the author and do not necessarily reflect the views of the publisher,
and the publisher hereby disclaims any responsibility for them.

Any people depicted in stock imagery provided by Thinkstock are models,
and such images are being used for illustrative purposes only.
Certain stock imagery © Thinkstock.

ISBN: 978-1-4897-1089-5 (sc)
ISBN: 978-1-4897-1088-8 (e)

Library of Congress Control Number: 2016920766

Print information available on the last page.

LifeRich Publishing rev. date: 3/13/2017

"American Child"

American child, does the call of the wild
Ever sing in the midst of your dreams?
And with the coming of dawn,
When you awake, and it's gone,
When it's over, do you know what it means?

Can you imagine a day,
When a man found his way,
Through a wild and an unbroken land?
That was before the machine,
Turned the blue and the green,
Into some color I can't understand.

**Excerpt from a poem written by James
G. Peck (The High-Country Man)**
of Beverly, WV

Looking northwest from Germany Valley in Pendleton County, WV

A NOTE FROM THE AUTHOR

My ancestors were among the first settlers in Pendleton County, West Virginia. I guess that's why I feel "rooted" here, like the Dyers in this book, and enjoy learning about the history, customs, and legends of the place I'm thankful to call home.

My mom, my husband, and I live in Kiser Gap on my homeplace which is near the sites of Fort Upper Tract and Fort Seybert, frontier forts built around 1756. In 1758, Shawnee and Delaware warriors, led by Delaware medicine man and war chief, Bemino (known by the settlers as John Killbuck, Sr.) led a raiding party to these forts. Although this book is fictional, many of the events throughout the story are based on written accounts of the raid on Fort Seybert.

As a third-grade teacher, I took my students on field trips to Fort Seybert during the Treasure Mountain Festival. This yearly festival is held to retain our local heritage and to commemorate events that happened at Fort Seybert in 1758. The beauty of the Fort Seybert area, along with the excitement of my students as they learned the fort's history inspired me to write this book. I was pleased to be asked to participate in the Fort Seybert massacre reenactment in 2016 during which I portrayed one of the settlers who was captured.

I enjoyed working on this project for the past several years, but I haven't done this alone! There are many people to thank for their support and guidance. I apologize to anyone I forgot to mention:

A special thank-you to Marshall Liskey and Joely Ferrell (Jed Conrad's granddaughter) in the front cover photo. Also thanks to their parents for allowing me to use this picture.

Doris Short (my mom), Sandra Propst (my aunt), Cindy Wilkins, Paula Waggy, and my last class of NFES third graders—editors and advice-givers.

Dean Hardman—Interpreter for "History Hitting the Road," an educational outreach program from the Historic Area at WVU Jackson's Mill.

The Killbuck Riflemen and other Fort Seybert Rendezvous participants who sparked interest, answered many questions, and taught my students and me so much throughout the years. This list includes: Jim Kile, Robert Nesselrodt, Dave Snyder, B.J. Bobby, John Affonso, Corey Taylor, Greg Cougevan, George Kinnison, Jack Hasselaar, Kurt Baier, and Jim Peck. There were others whose names I neglected to gather throughout the years.

Judy Wilson, Bradley Omanson, and Gene Conley—Interpreters at Prickett's Fort near Fairmont, West Virginia.

Randy Marcum—WV State Archives historian.

Jed Conrad (owner of site of Fort Seybert), Jake and Carol Conrad, Greg Adamson, Stanna Smith, Dewayne Borror, Morris Mallow, John Dalen, Patricia Boggs Alt, Harry Lee Temple, Richard Ruddle, Jr., David Earl Swecker, and Stanley Kile—for sharing your historical knowledge and relics with me.

Donald Mallow—for the trip across the river to the site of Fort Upper Tract.

Elwood Kile—patient husband (I'm finally finished with *this* book, but I have another one in the works!), chauffeur, and thesaurus.

As you read this book, I hope you can imagine being on the western Virginia (eastern West Virginia) frontier over 250 years ago!

To contact the author: rkile1963@gmail.com

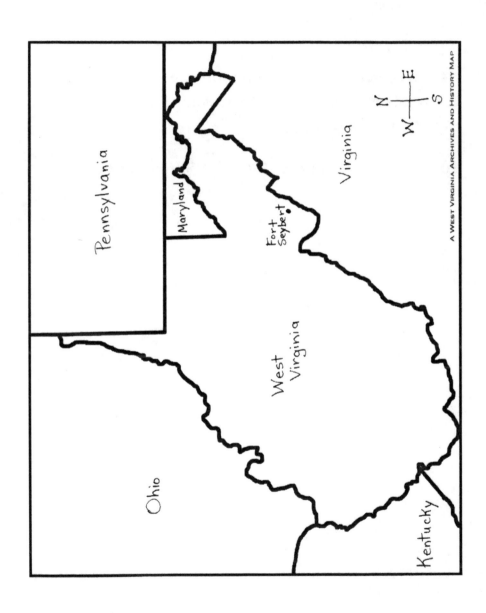

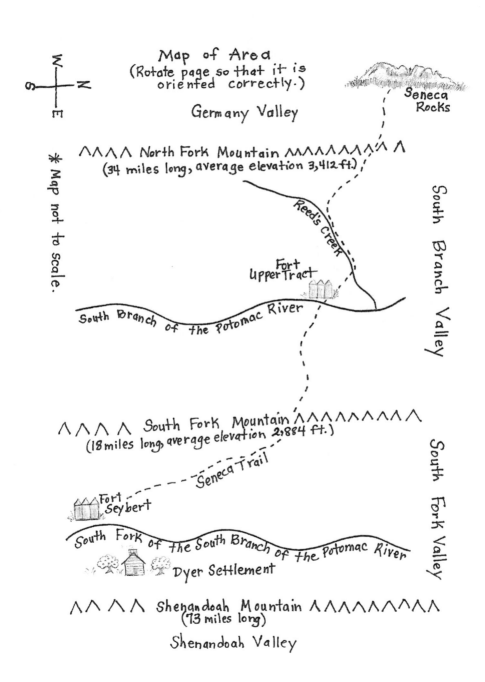

Map of Area
(Rotate page so that it is
oriented correctly.)

Germany Valley

Seneca Rocks

W N S E

✳ Map not to scale.

∧∧∧∧ North Fork Mountain ∧∧∧∧∧∧∧∧∧ ∧
(34 miles long, average elevation 3,412 ft.)

Reed's Creek

South Branch Valley

Fort Upper Tract

South Branch of the Potomac River

∧ ∧ ∧ ∧ South Fork Mountain ∧∧∧∧∧∧∧∧∧
(18 miles long, average elevation 2,884 ft.)

Seneca Trail

South Fork Valley

Fort Seybert

South Fork of the South Branch of the Potomac River

Dyer Settlement

∧∧ ∧ ∧ Shenandoah Mountain ∧∧∧∧∧∧∧∧
(73 miles long)

Shenandoah Valley

CHAPTER 1

"Wake up, Sarah!" James Dyer shook his nine-year-old sister's shoulder as he crawled past her and headed down the loft ladder. Sarah's unconscious brain was trying to understand what she had just heard. Suddenly, her eyes flew open. Mother had promised she and James could go fishing today! Her older brother was already dressed and down the peg ladder that led from the loft to the main floor of their small cabin. Sarah heard Mother's sweet voice below. "Good morning, James." James greeted Mother warmly in reply.

Sarah threw back her homemade comforter and nearly leapt from her corn-husk-stuffed mattress that lay on the floor. Although the loft ceiling was low, Sarah could stand erect if she stood in the middle of the room where the roofline was steeper. She stood there in her handmade shift and grabbed her linsey-woolsey dress and apron hanging from a wooden peg attached to one of the rafters. She hurriedly slipped the dress over her long brown braid and tied the apron around her waist. Soon she was downstairs, too.

"Good morning, sleepy head."

Sarah gave her mother a soft hug in reply. Then she sat down on the heavy, oak bench beside her brother. Mother placed a wooden bowl filled with cornmeal mush in front of each of her children. Sarah picked up her special spoon carved from buffalo horn and took her first bite. As the warm creamy substance crossed her tongue, she realized Mother had sweetened it with a touch of honey Father had harvested last summer from the bee skep beside their cabin. "Mmm, Mother, this is sooo good!" she said between spoonfuls.

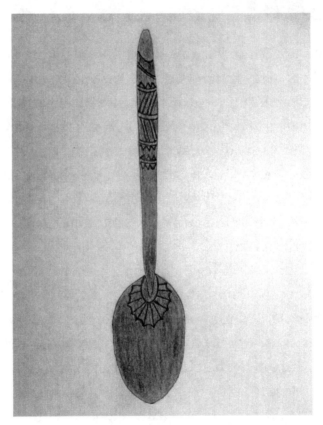

Carvings on the back of Sarah's spoon

"That's just about the last of the honey. I hope the apple trees are in full blossom this year so the bees can refill their hive. I'm sure they'll be willing to share some of it with us," replied Mother as she sat down across from the children with her own bowl of mush.

"Maybe next time Father will be able to get some honey without getting stung," added Sarah.

Mother nodded, "It's a good thing we had some bee balm growing in the garden to help with the pain and swelling. Those little guys really laid into him!"

James wasn't paying much attention to their conversation. His thoughts were on the trout he planned to catch after breakfast. "Are you going with us, Mother?" he asked.

"I wish I could," she replied, "but since your father is away, I have extra work to do around here."

"Are you sure you don't want us to stay and help you?" inquired James between bites, secretly hoping Mother's reply would be *no*.

"I promised you could go today. Besides, you stacked plenty of wood by the door and filled up the water buckets last evening, so I'm ready for the day," answered Mother. James's heart gave a leap. "You can both get back to your chores tomorrow."

"We'll work double hard for you then," declared James.

Sarah added, "Maybe you can go with us next time!" The children knew Mother enjoyed fishing with them and rarely let them go alone. She had made them promise to be careful. James knew Mother was counting on their faithful dog, Duke, to watch after them. In addition to being an excellent hunter, Duke was very protective of the children. He followed them wherever they went.

When James finished eating, he climbed back up to the loft. In the dim light, he crawled to a far corner and felt around until his hand touched a small, wooden box. He grabbed it and went back down the ladder. He placed the box on the table and opened it. Inside was a piece of cloth, some homemade bone hooks, and his meager supply of fishing line he had made from milkweed stem fibers. He wrapped the line and hooks in the piece of cloth and placed it inside his long-tailed, hunter's shirt above his leather belt. Then he set the empty box on the mantle. By this time, Sarah had finished her breakfast.

"Come on, Sarah. We need some worms." On the way out the door, James grabbed his sheathed tomahawk and attached it around his waist. Sarah followed her brother outside where Duke greeted them cheerfully. He put his paws up on Sarah's apron, and she rubbed his ears and stuck her nose against his wet one. James grabbed the gourd dipper hanging beside the door. He used it to dip out a cool drink of water from the bucket below it. Then he passed the dipper to his sister and rushed around the fenced-in garden to the back of the cabin. Duke followed him.

After Sarah got a drink, she, too, hurried behind the cabin where pieces of old wood and rocks were scattered about. The children knew these were the favorite hiding places of worms. Sarah squealed, "James come here!" each time she found one. She enjoyed looking for them, but couldn't bring herself to actually pull the slippery critters from the ground. James gently tugged on each one until it slurped free of the earth. Then he carefully placed the squirming worms in a small leather bag he had lined with moss to keep them moist and cool. As the children searched for bait, Duke ran around their feet sniffing at the pieces of wood. He wasn't looking for worms but was hoping for a ground squirrel to appear.

The tan, short-haired cur was a great hunter of ground squirrels, mice and all other small woodland creatures. One of his jobs was to keep the outside area around their cabin free of the pesky animals. This helped inside the house as well.

Cabin at Fort Seybert

Although Mother praised Duke for a job well done, he was never allowed in the house. *No respectable person would allow a dog inside his home,* she would say.

As soon as James had what he considered a sufficient amount of bait, he draped the flap over the pouch's opening. Then he put his head through the strap and crossed it over one shoulder. Grabbing the two, thin wooden poles propped against the side of the house, James was ready to go. Sarah was still on her knees searching for worms. "That's enough, Sarah," said James. Sarah jumped up and followed her brother.

"Bye, Mother," they both yelled as they happily ran past the cabin door. At that moment, Mother stepped out and called,

"Wait, children, I have some dinner for you!" She handed James a small sack which he tucked inside his shirt beside his fishing supplies. Mother also gave him his canteen which he quickly filled from one of the water buckets by the door.

"Thanks, Mother," the siblings replied as they hurried off.

"Goodbye, children. Please be careful," came Mother's worried command. "Duke, watch out for them!" she added as the dog happily trotted behind the children.

CHAPTER 2

The threesome headed west toward the river. James and Sarah hadn't been fishing in the Wappatomaka, the name the Indians had given the nearby river, since last fall. Fishing was good this time of year because the fish were hungry after the long winter spent under ice. The winters were very cold in this mountainous section of the Virginia frontier.

The children were anxious to drop their lines in the cold ripples of the river and hoped to snag a tasty meal. They were tired of living off winter meals of cornmeal mush, salted pork, deer jerky, turnips, and dried corn, beans, and pumpkin. Mother made these foods as tasty as she could, but everyone was ready for a treat of fresh fish. She had promised to fry their catch for supper this evening. Of course, since Father had left for the trading post yesterday, he would miss the feast.

The usual blanket of April fog had settled into the South Fork Valley overnight, but the fog couldn't hide the fact that spring was slowly taking hold of the land. Refreshing sights, sounds, and smells surrounded them as they walked toward the river. Along the path May-apples, blood root, and spring beauties poked their noses through the warming earth. Their green foliage was a stark contrast to last fall's brown leaves that carpeted the ground. Although the fog blocked the children's view of the mountains this morning, they knew the trees there were just beginning to leaf out, and the hidden woods were dotted with the tiny blossoms of the red buds. In the clearings near the edge of the forest, the Blackhaw trees were covered with clusters of white flowers, and the dogwoods were in full bloom.

As they passed the sugar grove, James noticed the maple limbs were also budding, and he thought of the sugar his family had made from the sap they'd collected from these trees in February. Some of the sugar had been pressed into little wooden molds. When they hardened, Mother had dumped the cakes out of the molds and had stored them in a cloth bag. James knew she would use these sugar cakes as treats for birthdays and other special occasions.

The sounds of the forest caught James's attention, too. Spring mornings sounded much busier than the cold silence of winter's daybreak. Song birds filled the woods with their cheerful melodies, squirrels chattered, and turkeys gobbled in the distance. James took a deep breath. The air smelled fresh and clean. This was his favorite time of year. Everything was waking up following the long, frigid winter, and it was exciting to be part of it.

James felt that he was "waking up" also. He was thirteen, and according to his father, now a man. He knew he was still a child in most people's eyes, especially his mother's, but his father had put James in charge of the homestead when he left. James recalled his father's words: *You're a man now, son, and I'm depending on you to take care of your mother and sister while I'm gone. If the alarm is sounded, get them to the fort quickly. There hasn't been any trouble with the Indians recently, but we must always be cautious.*

I'll take care of Mother and Sarah. You can rely on me, Father, James had proudly replied.

The three continued along the rocky path. James and Sarah had to avoid the occasional protruding rocks and roots on the trail. Duke, however, paid no mind to the obstacles. He was nimble enough to dodge them as he ran on his merry way, but the children were barefoot, and they definitely didn't want to stub a toe. An injury might ruin their day of fishing.

James recalled the bloody stubbed toe he'd received last spring while chasing a runaway sheep. Mother was trying to shear the ewe and the sheep was not enjoying the experience. The half-shorn sheep broke free and ran toward the woods. James was sure he could catch her...until his big toe on his right foot rammed into a jutting rock splitting the corner of his nail. James had doubled over in pain, the sheep forgotten.

Eventually the pain subsided, and he was able to hobble back to the house. After Mother cleaned the blood from his swollen toe, she placed a poultice of sweet everlasting leaves on it to help the pain. Later that day, the ewe had wandered back to their house. She looked rather comical with only half her wool. James caught the sheep, and Mother completed the shearing. James occasionally reminded that ewe that her adventure had unnecessarily caused him much pain.

The children had worn their moccasins throughout the winter, but had shed them just this morning. May first was the customary day of "the shedding of shoes," but the weather was warming quickly this spring so Mother had allowed them to go barefoot two days earlier than usual. The siblings knew going barefoot during the spring and summer made their father happy because he made their deer hide shoes. Not wearing them during the warm months made their moccasins last a little longer. Of course, they preferred to be without shoes anyway. They would remain barefoot all summer and into the fall until once again the ground became too cold for bare feet. The soles of their feet were a little tender this morning, but within a week, they would toughen.

As they continued along, James took a deep cleansing breath. It was so refreshing to have a "free" day. Much of the children's outdoor time was spent working near the cabin. Some of their chores were seasonal. In the spring and summer, the children were expected to help plant the corn, beans, pumpkins, gourds, squash, and flax. In addition, the woven twig fence that stood six feet out from two sides of their cabin had to be kept up. This fence kept their wandering livestock from eating the medicinal herbs and potherbs that grew there.

Fall brought hog butchering, harvesting, and corn grinding. Their favorite autumn job was to gather nuts. At that time of year, the woods around them were littered with black walnuts, butternuts, hazelnuts, chestnuts, and hickory nuts. In the winter, the children helped feed and water the sheep, milk cow, and chickens.

Of course, many chores were daily no matter the season. James thought of the hundreds, probably thousands of buckets of water he and Sarah had carried from the nearby spring to their cabin. He also made sure Mother had sufficient wood piled by their door. Even on the hottest of days, the fireplace needed fuel for cooking their meals. Today James was thankful he and Sarah didn't have to think about any chores!

Garden along cabin wall with herbs and bee skep

After walking about half a mile, the siblings were within earshot of the river, and the gentle roar of it called to them. Normally from here they would be able to see the stockade and blockhouse of the fort towering on the hill above them, but today it was hidden by the fog. The fort's presence was a constant reminder that the settlers were unwelcome on these once-abundant hunting and planting grounds of the Indians.

Soon the fishermen reached the river's bank near John Patton's Mill and looked down at the water below them. "Let me go first," James said. James held his pole high over his head as he scrambled down the slippery bank to the river's edge. Once there, he reached up for Sarah's pole and placed it on the ground beside his. He took Sarah's hand and helped her navigate down the slope. Duke had already raced ahead of them and was out of sight by the time Sarah reached the river. James called for him, and he splashed through the water to the children. Excitement showed in his rapidly wagging tail.

James quickly took the pouch out of his shirt and carefully removed some line and a sharp, bone hook. He attached the hook to the line, and then tied it to the end of Sarah's pole. Next, he took out a wriggling worm and speared it onto the waiting hook. He handed the pole to Sarah. Then he grabbed his pole from the ground and repeated the process. By the time he had gotten his hook baited, Sarah had already plopped hers into the cold water. James dropped his line in, too, and watched as it floated with the current. Again and again, they threw in their lines and watched them meander downstream. Eventually the worms had become limp and were no longer moving. Sarah became bored and said, "Nothin's bitin', James, let's go somewhere else."

"We haven't been here long," replied her brother. "Don't complain. They'll start bitin' soon. Here swing your hook over to me. I'll put on a fresh worm. That should help." But it didn't, and after a while, James was anxious for a tug on his line, too. "OK, Sarah, I'm ready to move on now, too. Let's try somewhere else." James jerked the lifeless worms off both hooks and tossed them into the moving water. Then the siblings twisted their lines around their wooden poles so they wouldn't get caught as they walked through the thick brush that grew along the river bank.

When Mother went fishing with them, they always headed

south as they fished, but today James headed north. Sarah noticed the change in direction but trusted her older brother to find a good spot. Duke really didn't care which way they went. There was always some new scent to excite him, and he would trail off up over the bank only to return after a few minutes to get a pat on the head and a few kind words as he checked on the children. In places, the river's edge went all the way to the steep bank, and the children had to wade through the frigid water. Their bare toes grew so cold they felt numb, but they didn't mind. Their parents had taught them an important lesson at a young age: *If you want something, you must work hard for it, even if it causes you discomfort.* They definitely wanted some fresh fish even if it meant frozen toes!

James enjoyed the thinking time fishing gave him. As they walked along, he thought of the fish and other wild animals around the settlement that were used by his family. His father had taught him how to butcher all the animals they killed. Some of the meat was eaten fresh. What couldn't be eaten right away was cut into strips and dried for jerky or cured with salt. The hides of the animals were dried and traded for items the settlers needed. Sometimes the deer hides were tanned to make leather for clothing, gloves, moccasins, and leather strips.

Some of the French trappers who passed through their settlement had learned the uses of many native plants from the Indians. This knowledge had been shared with the settlers. James knew which berries were safe to eat, which plants were poisonous, and which ones could be used for medicine. He knew the roots of many wild plants were used to cure ailments: ginseng was used for colds and fevers, skunk cabbage for toothaches, and cattail for burns.

Frontiersmen made many of the items they wore

The Dyers and other pioneers, had also brought many types of seeds with them from their homelands, including ones to plant for medicine. They planted mullein to use for curing coughs, dandelions for a spring tonic, and Queen Anne's lace to help heal infections.

In addition, one of the first things the settlers did when they moved to the frontier was to plant apple seedlings. James recalled the trees now growing near their cabin and hoped for some of the delicious fruit this fall. The Dyers had brought the seedlings from Lancaster County, Pennsylvania to Indian Old Fields where they had previously lived. When they moved upriver, Father dug up some of the smaller trees and brought them along. These transplanted trees had been slow to grow and hadn't yet produced fruit. Maybe, thought James, this would be the year they would bear. The Dyers knew this land was rich in resources and would eventually provide everything they needed to thrive.

Two hundred yards down river, James stopped and stated, "This looks like a good place." He was right this time. Soon, he and Sarah each caught a nice-sized fish. Of course, this wouldn't be enough for supper. It would take five more of the speckled trout to feed their family this evening. James could easily down three of the fish himself, and Sarah and Mother would probably eat two apiece. Since Father was away, they wouldn't need quite as many as they usually did. Father had a big appetite and could eat at least five by himself! As he fished, James allowed his thoughts to remain on Father.

He had gone east across the Shenandoah Mountain with most of the other grown men—except for the elderly ones—of the Dyer Settlement. They would be gone for a couple of weeks. For the men, the winter of 1757-58, like all winters, had been spent hunting and trapping game. The pelts from the buffalo, elk, deer, foxes, beavers, rabbits, wildcats, and raccoons they'd killed had been fleshed and dried. Spring was the time to trade the furs. The men had loaded them onto their horses and headed for a trading post in the Shenandoah Valley. The furs would be exchanged for needed supplies: salt, sugar, flour, black powder, blocks of lead for bullet making, vinegar, dried fruits, and iron for making tools at the forge.

Animal pelts

It was a joyous time when the men returned from their trip. Father always surprised James and Sarah with a gift. One year, he brought them a bag of dried apple snits. The tangy dried fruits were quite a treat. The pieces of apple were tasty, but the best part of all was that Mother had made a delicious apple snit pie from some of them!

Last year, when Father had come home from his trading expedition, he had brought each of his children a special treasure—a bright blue, glass bead on a string of leather. *Beads like this are valuable to the Indians. They've traded many beaver pelts to trappers in exchange for beads like these,* their Father had told them. James and Sarah cherished the round glass beads and always wore them dangling from their necks. Sarah enjoyed rolling the smooth, cool sphere between her fingers, pondering the places and people the bead had encountered on its way to her.

James wondered what surprise Father would bring him when he returned this year. He secretly hoped it would be a new tomahawk. The blade on the one James had hanging by his side was chipped and the handle had been replaced twice. When James was a child, he had used the tomahawk for things that it shouldn't have been used for such as digging in the dirt and chipping at rocks.

The boys in the settlement also made a game of throwing their tomahawks at targets. This improved their aim and got them ready for the day they were given a rifle, but it sure didn't help the tomahawk's appearance. Although James used their grindstone to keep his tomahawk sharp, the blade was slowly wearing down. Now that he was "grown" he would take better care of a new one. He had reminded his father of this before he left for the trading post.

A movement of his line brought James's attention back to fishing. James jerked the pole, but immediately realized he had missed his catch. The children continued fishing as they headed down river. They still only had the two fish, but the occasional nibbles they got fueled their enthusiasm. They knew the fish were there; they just had to be patient.

Even though Mother had made them bring a canteen of water along, the children preferred drinking from the river. As they walked along, they occasionally stopped, got on their hands and knees, and took a long, cold drink from the flowing water. Mother had told them it was "uncivilized" to drink water this way, but James and Sarah thought it was fun. They enjoyed mimicking Duke and the wild animals of the forest.

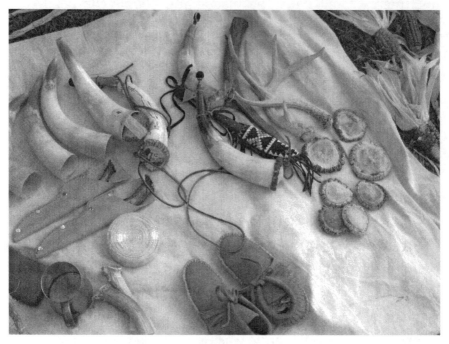

Trade goods

After a couple of hours of walking and fishing downstream, Sarah began to feel a little uneasy and spoke up, "James, we've come a long way. Maybe we should head back home."

"Don't worry, Sarah. I know where I'm going. I was down here with Nicholas one day last year, and he showed me a place where the fish congregate." Sarah's thoughts wandered to Nicholas, the son of Jacob Seybert. Jacob was the captain of the local militia. Captain Seybert was a respected man in their community as was his fourteen-year-old son. Both of them had proven leadership abilities. Sarah had renewed hope they would catch more fish if they went to Nicholas's spot.

"Come on, Duke," said James. On hearing his name mentioned the mutt raced through the water toward James for a nice head rub. Then the three of them continued walking north.

CHAPTER 3

Still somewhat reluctant, Sarah followed her brother farther and farther down river. By now the warm sun had burned off the fog, and its rays shone through the trees causing the river to glisten. Huge, ancient sycamores stood above them. Sarah pretended the trees' curved, white limbs were giant arms protecting her and James. She picked up a few large pieces of the blotchy gray and tan bark that had shed from the trees and tucked them inside her apron pocket. She would practice her handwriting on them using charred pieces of wood from the fireplace. Mother had been teaching her how to make the fancy letters, and Sarah enjoyed writing them.

There were no schools in their settlement, so in addition to handwriting, Mother had also taught the children to read using the worn, family *Bible*, the only book they owned. The children's great-grandmother and great-grandfather Dyer had given the special book to James and Sarah's grandparents before they left their native country to sail to this new land called America. The *Bible* had been passed down to their father. Mother read to the family from it every night before they went to bed. Sarah smiled as she recalled valuable lessons she had learned from those stories. She'd know how to tame lions and conquer giants if she ever encountered either of them. She had also learned if she disobeyed she might be swallowed by a whale. This thought concerned Sarah until Father chuckled and told her the ocean was very far away.

The *Bible* was precious to their family. Mother had often told her children, *We have many family members across the ocean. When they read aloud from their Bible, and I read to you from this one, the scriptures float gently through the air. They meet in the middle of the wide sea to create a bridge. In this way, our family is always connected no matter where we are living.*

Sarah felt this connection deeply, especially when she read the family names and birthdates lovingly written inside the front cover of their *Bible*. Although she knew she would probably never have the opportunity to visit her far-away family, she still yearned to see them. She imagined she knew them and had conversations with them in her mind. Their voices were kind and gentle. She hoped they could visualize her, too. Could they picture her long, brown hair and see that she had inherited her mother's shining blue eyes?

They continued walking down river. Sarah's thoughts trailed back to the day at hand when she noticed little bunches of fawn-colored fluff floating through the air. "What's this?" she asked James as she captured some in her hand and held it out for him to see.

"It's from the button balls on the sycamore trees," he replied as he pointed up into the tops of the trees. "They're seeds." Sarah tipped her head back as far as she could and looked straight up. The leaves on the trees were still very small, so she could see the round seed pods hanging on the highest limbs. James continued explaining, "The pods break apart in the spring and the fluff makes the seeds light so the wind can carry them. Then the seeds land on the water and are carried downstream to be deposited all along the bank. That's why there are so many sycamore trees along the river here."

As she walked along, Sarah studied the seed in her hand and thought it would be exciting to be tiny enough to float on the fluff and sail on the water to places unknown. Her father had told her once about the mouth of this river and the large bay into which it emptied, the Chesapeake. Perhaps one day she could float like the sycamore seeds to that bay. From there she could sail across the Atlantic and visit her far-away family. That idea made her smile.

Sarah's thoughts were interrupted when James stopped and said, "We're here." Sarah peered at an enormous spot in the water where the river seemed to stand still. The dark color of the water proved it was deep. Sarah hoped James was right, and it would be filled with shiny trout. Once again he baited their hooks. It didn't take long to discover this deep water was teeming with fish. Soon, between them, they had snagged five more of the speckled creatures.

"We have enough fish now, James. Let's go," encouraged Sarah.

"I'll have to get some sticks first," replied her brother as he walked near one of the sycamore trees and looked around on the ground until he found two nice-sized forked branches. He used his worn tomahawk to fashion them into fish-carrying sticks. Then he picked up each fish and pushed the end of the stick opposite the fork through one gill and out each fish's mouth. James put the two smaller fish on one twig and the five larger ones on the other. The forks at the bottom of the sticks kept the fish from sliding off. Then James handed the stick with two fish to Sarah. "Do you think you can carry these?" he asked her.

"I think so," she replied, taking the twig from his hand and lifting it high enough to keep the fork from touching the ground. James whistled for Duke who came running. Since they were no longer fishing, they didn't have to follow the river, so they took a shorter route home. They crawled up over the bank and headed southeast through the woods. Sarah now felt more at ease knowing they were headed homeward. As they left the riverbank, James briefly stopped at a birch tree. The catkins on its flimsy branches were blowing in the slight breeze. He broke off two thin twigs and stripped off the small leaves and flower clusters. Then he handed one small branch to Sarah. The siblings stuck the twigs in their mouths and gnawed off the thin bark while they continued along. As they chewed the bark, the delicious taste of wintergreen filled their mouths.

"There's one more thing we need to do before we go home," said James. "I want to dig some sassafras roots for Mother. There's a stand nearby." When they reached the special trees, James used his tomahawk to dig into the rocky soil to get some of the finger-sized roots. He knew this would probably damage his tomahawk even more but was hopeful Father would replace it soon.

Once the roots were unearthed and cut free, James wiped them across his breeches to remove the dirt. The dark orange color and pungent odor proved they were sassafras. He then chopped them into six-inch lengths and tucked them inside his shirt. They felt cool against his warm skin. The spicy scent filled his nostrils as they walked on. James knew their mother would brew some delicious tea from these roots. The tasty tea would be perfect with the fish this evening. The thought of food made James's mouth salivate.

Tomahawks

He looked skyward. The sun was already west of overhead signaling it was past their dinnertime. "Are you hungry, Sarah?" he asked his sister.

"I was hoping we could eat soon," she replied. "I didn't want to tell you I was hungry. I was afraid you would think I was complaining again. I know you don't like it when I complain."

James flipped Sarah's braid and grinned. "Let's find a good place to eat and see what Mother packed for us."

"OK, James, but let's eat fast. I'm ready to get home." The children sat down by a large white oak, and James pulled the small food sack from his shirt. He opened it and took out three strips of deer jerky and two Johnny cakes. James handed one of the cakes and a strip of jerky to Sarah. Duke came running toward them when he smelled the food. James gave the hungry dog his portion, and he eagerly wolfed it down in one bite. Then he begged both children for more. "Sorry, Duke," said Sarah. "You'll have to go find a ground squirrel or a mouse to eat if you're still hungry." Not understanding, Duke nosed the fish lying on the ground between them but was scolded by James for that. Sensing that he was getting no more food, the mutt took off on the hunt once again.

James and Sarah whispered as they ate. They had been taught to be quiet when they were in the woods. Animal watching was a favorite pastime of the children, and they knew if they wanted to see any game they must talk softly. Sometimes, when they were exploring near their home, they saw beautiful white-tailed deer grazing along the edge of the forest. The deer were pretty skittish around the settlement because they had learned that people were dangerous. The children had also heard and seen enormous elk. Their bugling echoed across the hills and valleys in the fall. The woods and clearings were filled with rabbits, squirrels, and grouse. Occasionally, they also saw black bears. Father had told them there weren't as many woods buffalo here as there used to be, but they enjoyed watching the small herd that sometimes grazed on the tall, bluejoint grass that grew in the valley. The family had even named their bottomland "The Buffalo Meadows" after the large, hairy beasts.

The siblings kept their voices down so they could see the animals, but they kept quiet for another reason, too. Indians! James and Sarah had only seen a few of the dark-skinned men, but they'd heard of settlers who'd been harmed by them. Indians hadn't been seen in these parts for a while, and the settlers hoped they would never return. However, Indians were always in the back of everyone's mind, and now they crept to the front of Sarah's.

She quietly spoke between bites, "James, will we always have to worry about Indians coming here?"

"Are you thinking about them again, Sarah? Don't worry! Father says as soon as more settlers move here, the Indians will stop coming. They stopped growing crops here a long time ago. They have other hunting grounds, too, so Father thinks they'll be able to find their game elsewhere. The only Indians who come here now are small groups of raiding parties that occasionally pass through, but Duke will let us know if there are any strangers nearby."

"I hope the Indians never come back. Why did our parents move to the frontier, anyway?" Sarah questioned. "If they knew the Indians were here, why did they come?"

"Father wanted his own land," explained James. "He wanted to be a farmer, and when he had the opportunity to come to the frontier, he knew his dream had come true. When he and Mother moved to the Indian Old Fields north of here, he thought that was the answer to his dream. But, that land turned out to be too swampy. A few years later, he bought this tract of over 1,000 acres and we moved up river."

"I wonder if Father believes moving here was the right thing to do?" asked Sarah. "I mean it's been such hard work getting the land cleared of rocks and trees, and I know he must worry about keeping us safe."

"You know Father isn't afraid of hard work. I think he worries about the Indians at times, but he still believes in what he's doing. He thinks we'll be able to make a good life here. This British settlement is growing, and many nationalities are represented here: Germans, British, Scotch, Irish. Father said even though our customs and languages are different, everyone has different skills they can use to help the whole community. We have to depend on each other since there aren't any towns around here. We have a lot of neighbors in these parts, and we also have the fort to keep us safe if the Indians do come back. Don't worry, Sarah. We're safe."

Sarah and James were finishing their last bite of jerky when Duke ran to them. He was whining and seemed anxious to move on. "Let's go, James," insisted Sarah. "I think Duke's trying to tell us something. Anyway, Mother will be worried if we aren't back soon."

James handed Sarah his canteen and she quickly took a drink and handed it back to her brother. James took a swig, too. Then they grabbed their poles and fish and continued on. Sarah tried to walk fast, but the going was slow now that she had fish to tote along. James had to walk slower than usual, too. Duke was the only one who could travel quickly, and Sarah had to constantly call him back to them.

The three continued on toward their cabin. Finally, after several stops to rest, they were nearing home. All at once, Sarah detected a strong odor that stopped her in her tracks. She rested the forks of her fish-carrying stick on the ground. "James, something's on fire," she said fearfully. Duke had also noticed the scent, and the fur along his spine rose.

"It's just coming from our chimney. The air is probably drawing the smoke this way. I'm sure Mother has a fire built in the fireplace to fry these fine fish we caught," James replied, trying to reassure his sister as well as himself. As the smoke became thicker, however, James realized it was more than just chimney smoke. Duke was now walking close to James's heels.

"I think the woods are on fire. Keep your eyes sharp,"

cautioned James. "We may have to detour around it to get home." They carefully walked on but saw no flames, so they picked up their pace. Soon the smoke began to dissipate and their fears subsided. *Maybe it was just smoke from their chimney,* hoped James. In a few minutes, their cabin was in sight. Oddly though, no smoke spiraled from the chimney as they expected. James quickened their pace. Upon reaching their home, they dropped the fish on the ground beside the door and raced inside. The windows had been shuttered, and the room was dim. James knew this was very unusual on such a beautiful spring day. The cabin was only one room with the small loft overhead, and they didn't see their mother, nevertheless Sarah called, "Mother, we're back! Where are you?"

There was no reply.

"Where is she?" asked Sarah, worry creeping into her voice.

James tried to comfort his sister. "She's probably outside gathering dandelion greens from the side garden. You know she always likes to fix a mess of greens this time of year to purify our blood."

"She would have heard me and answered if she was there," Sarah replied as she turned toward the door. Just then her keen eyes spotted a note lying on the table. She quickly picked it up, held it in the light from the doorway, and read it aloud:

> *Indians spotted nearby. Couldn't find you at the river. I pray you heard the alarm and are safe at the fort. I am headed there. Come quickly, but quietly. Be careful. I love you both.*
>
> *Mother*

CHAPTER 4

Panic gripped the children. James felt a tightening in his chest, and a shiver went up Sarah's spine causing the fine hairs at the base of her neck to stand on end.

Immediately, James recalled his father's command, *I'm depending on you to take care of your mother and sister while I'm gone.*

"We'd better hurry. Come on, Sarah!" He dropped the note and they rushed outside.

"What about Duke?" yelled Sarah, as the dog ran from the back of the house to join them. James grabbed Duke by the scruff of his neck and pushed him inside the house.

"We have to leave him here. He might bark if he sees an Indian. He'll be fine until we get back."

"But Mother never lets Duke in the house, and he doesn't have any food or water!" exclaimed Sarah.

Her brother hurriedly grabbed a half-full water bucket and sat it in the house for Duke. Then James quickly closed the door. "Mother won't mind if we leave him in here just this once, Sarah. This is an emergency! He'll be fine. I'll sneak back and get him later."

Chapter 4

The children ran as quickly and quietly as they could around the edge of the meadow. Soon, they were on the narrow path that led to the fort. James and Sarah knew the path well. Their parents had made them practice to be sure they could navigate it quickly and quietly. They had frequently made a game of following it. Being a little taller with longer legs, James slowed his pace so Sarah wouldn't get too far behind.

Within a few minutes they were nearing the fort. They couldn't see it yet, but James could picture it in his mind. It was a two-story, twenty-foot-square blockhouse inside a circular stockade of ten-foot high sharpened poles. The enclosure was big enough for everyone in the settlement.

At the end of the path, they stopped abruptly before leaving the safety of the trees. As they caught their breath, they smelled smoke once again. Peering through some low-hanging limbs, they couldn't believe what was before them. They saw the fort—or what was left of it—just a tall, stone chimney standing above a pile of smoldering logs. On the flag pole, the British flag, once red, white, and blue, now looked like a piece of tattered char cloth flapping in the breeze. The only other movement they could see was an occasional robin hopping in the short grass near the fort's remains. A few of the stockade logs still stood, but they were badly charred. Occasionally one of them would send poofs of gray smoke into the bright, blue sky. Sarah and James were unable to comprehend the sight. What had happened here?

James's mind raced. This had been their safe place. When Indians were spotted nearby, one of the men of the settlement would ride through the area on horseback alerting everyone of the danger. Then the settlers would grab the supplies they

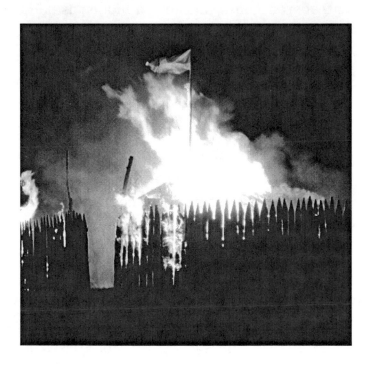

needed for a few weeks and hurry here to "fort up" until the danger passed. Father always said, *We'll be fine if we all remain together,* and the children had felt safe in the fort the few times they had been alerted to go. Now the fort was gone. James and Sarah stared in awe at the horrible sight. Sarah began crying quietly. "Oh, James, was Mother in there?" she asked between sobs.

"I don't know, Sarah, but I have to go see if I can find anyone. You stay hidden here. You can watch me, and if there is danger, run back to the cabin and stay inside with Duke." Sarah looked at her brother fearfully. Tears streamed down her face. She didn't like the idea of James going near the fort, but she did so want to see her mother. Maybe Mother was hiding somewhere in the woods near the fort, as they were. If she saw James, she would make herself known to him. Sarah shook her head in agreement, obeyed James, and stayed hidden as he'd told her to do.

James nervously looked around before stepping into the open. Seeing no one, he crouched low as he crossed the river on the log bridge. Then he quickly scrambled past the mill and up the bank toward the fort. In a few minutes he reached it and cautiously stepped through the opening where the gate once stood. Once "inside" the fort, he was heartbroken. It felt as if he was somewhere else—somewhere he'd never been before. Nothing looked familiar. His heart beat rapidly as his eyes darted in all directions hoping to find his mother—anyone—but he saw no one. The odor of smoke surrounded him as he surveyed the damage. The blockhouse had collapsed. All that was left besides the stone chimney was a heap of burned logs. It didn't take long for James to realize Mother was not there, but where could she be? What about everyone else from the settlement? If the alarm had been sounded, there should have been at least forty people gathered inside. Since most of the men were away, there were less people in the area than usual, but where were they?

Leaving the confines of the fort, James headed outside the gate and walked the circumference of the stockade. He had to watch each step, not wanting to accidentally place his foot on a hot coal. Soon he had completed the circle and was back at the gate. A feeling of defeat overwhelmed him. He hadn't found anything. He still didn't know where Mother was. Frustration brought stinging tears to his eyes, but he knew he couldn't allow himself to cry. He needed to stay strong for Sarah. James shook his head and forced the tears away.

He turned homeward, and suddenly something unusual caught his eye. It was lying a few feet away from one of the blackened stockade posts. As his eyes focused on the object, he saw that it was a brown and white feather. He walked over to it, stooped, and immediately knew what it was attached to— an arrow. The shaft was partially buried in the ground with the feathers protruding. James slowly pulled the arrow from the damp earth. The sharp dark point was covered in dirt. He wiped it across his breeches, realizing what it must mean. His heart pounded in his ears as fear gripped him. James knew some of the Indians now had guns, but others still used bows and arrows. Indians *had* been here. They had done this horrible thing, but where were his mother and the other settlers? James quickly dropped the arrow to the ground. He didn't want Sarah to see it and become even more terrified than she already was.

James hurriedly ran down over the bank toward the river. He kept glancing back over his shoulder. He was sure he would see an Indian trailing him as he sprinted across the bridge to the safety of the woods. The dense trees made him feel more secure. He ran to the large tree where he had left Sarah. She stood there sniffling and immediately asked, "Did you find Mother?"

"No, I didn't find anyone," James answered breathlessly.

"I saw you pick up something. What was that, James?"

"Oh, nothing," he replied between breaths. "It was just a feather from a hawk. Come on. We need to get home." James tugged his sister's arm.

Sarah jerked away from him. "I'm not leaving without Mother!" she insisted.

"Mother's not here, Sarah. Maybe she's back home by now, but if not, I promise I'll find her. Now, come on!"

Sarah heard the urgency in James's voice and obeyed, hopeful he was right about Mother being at home. The two of them dashed back to the cabin without speaking. Unaware of their anxiety, Duke happily greeted them as they threw open the door. Much to their disappointment, Mother still wasn't there. Sarah immediately climbed the peg ladder to the loft, and James could hear her crying.

Duke didn't understand what was happening, but being inside the cabin was a new experience for him. He paced around the small room and finally plopped down in front of the door. James pulled in the door latch, which locked the door, and sat on one of the wooden benches by the table. He was overwhelmed with worry. What could he do?

Afternoon turned into evening and evening to night. Darkness enveloped the small cabin. Duke whined to be let out, and James reluctantly opened the door for him. James knew the dog could fend for himself and would bark if anyone was about. Of course, James was still hopeful at any moment to hear Mother's voice at the door. *Where could she be? Did the Indians take her and the others away? Why would they do that? And where would they take them?* He couldn't stop the questions swirling around in his mind.

CHAPTER 5

Sarah's crying had stopped. She'd obviously fallen asleep. Duke was still outside, and James hadn't heard him bark at all. That meant no one was nearby so James felt safe enough to partially open the shutter on one of the windows. Thankfully the moon was bright in the sky, and light streamed through the narrow opening.

Now James could walk around inside the cabin without stumbling. He knew it was important to keep up his strength because he planned to go looking for his mother the next morning. He went to the fireplace and swiveled the blackened, iron pot around on its hook. He didn't want to call attention to their cabin in case there were still some Indians nearby, so he didn't build a fire. He ladled some of the cold leftover turnips into his wooden bowl. As he did this, he thought of the prize catch of fish that lay outside on the ground. They were probably being enjoyed by Duke, but James didn't care. The fish didn't matter anymore. Only finding Mother mattered now. He sat in his mother's chair and ate slowly unaware of the bitter taste of the turnips.

If he was lucky, Sarah wouldn't wake until midmorning tomorrow. She was a late sleeper which usually peeved James, but now he considered it a blessing. He planned to go back to the fort at first light and look for more clues. He hoped to return before Sarah awakened.

After he finished eating, he shuttered the window and felt his way through the darkness to the table. He plopped down on one of the hard benches beside it. Then he crossed his arms on the table and dropped his head atop them. He was exhausted and sleep came quickly, but it wasn't restful. His dreams haunted him: feathered warriors hiding behind dark trees; Mother calling for help; Father telling him to take care of Mother and Sarah while he was gone. James woke often throughout the night with his heart pounding in fear.

Interior of frontier home

It was early morning when James was startled awake by sniffing outside the door. A quiet whine and scratching told him it was Duke. James opened the door for the dog and allowed him to enter. Then James quickly shut and locked the door. He petted the dog on his furry head. "Where's Mother, Duke?" he quietly asked the confused mutt. Duke's soft eyes had no answer and once again James sat down on one of the hard benches. Duke paced for a time and then quieted down by the door. James was anxious for daylight. He walked to one of the windows and opened the shutter every few minutes. As soon as the sky gave forth enough light to navigate, he wrote a hurried note to Sarah in case she awoke earlier than usual this morning. He knew he needed to travel fast, so he quietly pulled on his moccasins and crept out the heavy wooden door. Duke tried to follow him, but James pushed the dog back inside. He hoped Duke would be a comfort to Sarah if she woke up before he returned.

James quickly ran across the meadow to the path. As he crossed the log bridge and drew nearer the fort, the acrid, smoky odor met him again. The heavy morning mist had trapped the scent close to the ground. With each step it became stronger. As he approached the fort, he glanced around cautiously. Two deer grazed peacefully nearby, so sensing no danger, James stepped into the clearing. The deer snorted and fled toward the safety of the trees at the edge of the meadow.

This time, James decided to walk down over the bank toward the spring that supplied water for the settlers when they stayed at the fort. As he neared the pool of clear water, his eyes caught sight of something odd. In the dim light, James could barely make it out. Drawing closer, he knew what it was. More feathers! Walking toward them, he noticed these were not attached to an arrow like the ones he had found yesterday. These were bound together with a leather strap. James stooped to take a closer look. Beside the bunch of feathers, he saw something that made his stomach churn. Blood! A puddle the size of a plate painted the ground dark red. The short greening grass still held some of the sticky substance on its blades. Fear seized James and paralyzed him for a moment. His mind told him to run, but he couldn't. He stared at the blood praying it did not belong to his mother but then quickly realized it probably belonged to the wearer of the feathers.

When he finally got his wits about him, he walked back up to the fort to continue his search. Finding nothing outside the wall, he went inside again. He knew if people had been in there, they would have had supplies. Of course, some of the items like the bedding and clothing would have been consumed by the flames, but the cooking pots, skillets, iron utensils, guns, and knives should still be identifiable. He couldn't find any of those things. James knew this was very strange. Maybe some of it could be hidden beneath the large pile of charred logs but not everything!

James kicked some of the pieces of blackened wood to the side as he searched. There was no obvious evidence that anyone had been here at all. Hopeful thoughts sprang into his heavy heart. *Maybe the other settlers are safe in their homes! Maybe Mother fled to a neighbor's cabin! Maybe the Indians burned the fort before the settlers got here!* Immediately, though, the negative thoughts pushed out the positive ones. *What about the arrow… and the blood…and the feathers? And why hasn't Mother come home by now? No, I will think positively! Mother is fine!* Then he willed himself to speak out loud: "MOTHER IS SAFE AND I WILL FIND HER!"

CHAPTER 6

James's feet barely touched the ground as he ran up the rocky mountainside to the west of the fort. He knew the nearest cabin belonged to a family by the name of Conrad. When he reached it, he didn't bother knocking, barging into the home as if it were his own. He realized the homeowners would forgive such disrespect during an emergency such as this, but he needn't have worried about that, for the house stood empty. He then ran to each of the other houses scattered within a few miles of each other and the fort remains. He only stopped to rest when his lungs felt like they were ready to burst. Then he would bend over or fall to the ground and suck in the air as fast as he could—his heart pounding in his ears and his chest heaving up and down.

As soon as he regained a little strength, he pushed on to the next house and the next. Sadly, he found no one. Each empty house increased his worry and diminished his hope. It seemed as though everyone except him and his sister had vanished. Fear overwhelmed him and gripped his heart even tighter than the lack of air did. His head was spinning, and he felt light-headed. He and Sarah were in the settlement alone. What would he tell her when he got home?

James wasn't sure what to do next. Worried and exhausted, he headed toward their cabin. His imagination was as vivid as it had been the day before, forcing him to look over his shoulder as he hurried along. *Is someone following me? Is that an Indian behind that tree?* He raced across the log bridge and turned in the direction of the fort as he caught his breath and assured himself that no one was following him.

The sun had just topped Shenandoah Mountain when he reached home and pensively walked inside. Maybe, if Sarah still slept, he would have time to process all he had seen and formulate a plan. A plan to fix things. A plan to get everything back to normal.

Thankfully, Sarah was still asleep as James quietly entered their home. Duke greeted him with a whine and a wagging tail. James rubbed the dog's head and whispered a soft greeting to him as Duke ran outside.

Spinning wheel

James closed the door and sank down on one of the long benches. He looked around the small room at reminders of his mother. They filled every space. The stocky, rectangular table in front of him was where the family ate Mother's home-cooked meals together. Here and there on the wall hung gourd dippers and various household tools Mother used daily. The family's assortment of pewter and wooden plates, bowls, and cups sat on a shelf near the southern window. Below it, on a small table, were knives and a few wooden spoons and ladles. This table was where mother fixed simple but delicious meals from the salt pork, deer, squirrel, turkeys, and potherbs—fresh or dried depending on the season.

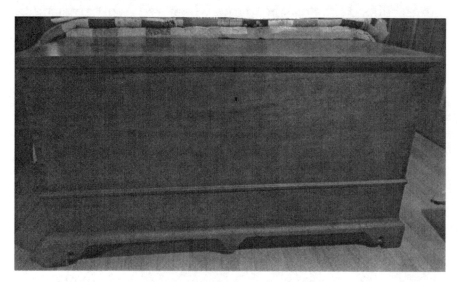

Blanket chest

Hanging from wooden pegs on the rafters were some of Mother's medicinal herbs and small bags of dried berries, nuts, seeds, and jerky. On the northern wall was another small window. By it were Mother's spinning wheel and a basket of unspun wool, probably sheared from that ole toe-busting ewe.

A stone fireplace was built on the western wall. It was here that Mother baked or cooked using the blackened iron pots and skillets stored on the hearth. A walnut blanket chest holding her few precious mementoes sat to the left of the fireplace. This was where Mother kept the family *Bible*. In his mind, James could hear his Mother's voice tenderly reading scriptures to the family.

A linen sampler with "Dyer" lovingly stitched in red thread sat on the mantle above the fireplace. Mother had embroidered it years ago when they'd first moved to the frontier. She'd used many bedstraw roots to dye the thread for the letters. Beside the sampler, a dark brown, stoneware pitcher held some wilted dogwood blossoms. It was a small and simply furnished cabin, but it was cozy. The Dyer family loved their little home, but it just wouldn't be a home without Mother.

Stoneware pitcher

James shook his head to clear that thought and fight the tears. *Mother will be back. When Father gets home, he'll find her,* James assured himself silently. But his father had only been gone one day. He wouldn't be back for a couple of weeks! That would be too long. He couldn't wait for Father to fix this. It might be too late by then. It was his duty to take care of the family now. He had promised Father. *He* would have to find Mother.

James's thoughts were interrupted when he heard shuffling overhead. He knew any moment Sarah would poke her head over the loft floor. What would he say to her? Usually, at this time of day, Mother would be there preparing breakfast. Sarah would be expecting this.

Momentarily, his prediction was realized as Sarah showed her face and rubbed her eyes trying to focus in the dim light. Her blue eyes widened as she realized their mother was still not home, and the tears once again began to flow. James knew he had to reassure her somehow, but he wanted to cry, too. His friend Wallace immediately came to mind. In an instant, James recalled what had happened: He and Wallace were cracking black walnuts with the hammer end of their tomahawks. James had placed a walnut on top of a rock and was steadying it between his index finger and thumb. When he slammed the hammer down to crack the nut, he accidentally hammered the side of his index finger, smashing it instead of the walnut. The tears had immediately stung his eyes, but Wallace had told James he was too old to cry so he didn't.

James knew he had to be brave for his younger sister. She was only nine and still allowed to cry. Of course, according to Wallace's teenage wisdom, girls were allowed to cry even if they were old and gray. If only his friend were here right now to give James more of his sage advice. Maybe Wallace could tell him what to do. Unfortunately, James knew he was on his own this time.

By now Sarah was down the ladder. She sat on the bench beside her brother. Tears were running down her cheeks. "I'm sure Mother will be home soon," James reassured the young girl. He dared not tell his sister about the puddle of blood he'd found earlier at the fort, as he knew that would increase her worry. He kept that "little" detail to himself but knew what he must tell her. "Sarah, I think Mother and the other settlers were captured by the Indians. I have to go find them."

A wide-eyed Sarah faced her brother. "Oh no, James! What will happen to Mother?" Then suddenly realizing James would be leaving, too, she quickly added, "You can't leave me here alone! I'm going with you!" Her crying became more intense as she bowed her head and held it in her hands.

James dropped to his knees on the floor in front of her. "Look at me, Sarah," he said softly. Sarah's head rose as he spoke directly to her. "You have to stay here, and you won't be alone. I'll leave Duke with you. Mother might come home and you have to be here to tell her where I am. Father won't know where I am if he gets home before I do, either."

"We'll leave a note," Sarah immediately replied, now feeling a wave of nausea come over her. "You can't leave me here, James," she repeated with quivering lips. "The Indians might come and get me, too!"

"I don't think they'll be back."

"How do you know that?"

"I just don't think they will," James firmly stated. "The fort is gone, and they probably think they got everyone. They don't have any reason to come back."

"I'm still afraid to stay here, James! Please don't go without me! Even with Duke here, I'll still be afraid!" Sarah held her head in her hands and sobbed.

James sighed. He understood the fear his sister was feeling. He was also fearful but couldn't let his sister know. That would just make this whole situation harder for her.

"OK, Sarah," said James reluctantly, "You can go, but you can't complain, and you have to keep up with me."

Sarah lifted her head and looked at James. "I promise," she replied as she sniffed her red nose and dried her tears with her apron tail.

"All right then, let's get things ready to go," ordered her brother. "We have to hurry. Mother's getting farther away from us all the time."

It made both children feel better to have a plan. Sarah began packing food. She stood on a stool and took down sacks of deer jerky, dried berries, and nuts from the rafters. She placed handfuls of them along with some left-over Johnny cakes in an empty sack. Mother always kept some hard tack on hand for Father's hunting trips, and Sarah added several squares of this to the sack, too. Last, she put in four of Mother's precious sugar cakes and then tied the sack closed with a strip of leather she had pulled from a peg on the wall.

While Sarah had been packing the food, James had gone to the loft and put on his buckskins. The leather pouch over his shoulder now held a small tin containing his flint, steel, flax fibers, and char cloth. The worms and moss had been tossed out the door. He had also taken a square of cloth from Mother's sewing basket. Then he had broken off small sprigs of a few of the dried medicinal herbs hanging from the rafters. These had been carefully wrapped inside the cloth.

"The food's ready, James," announced Sarah as she placed the pack on the table. James put the wrapped medicine on the table beside it.

"Good. Now go put on your moccasins. Get our blankets, too. It gets chilly outside at night this time of year." Sarah could hear the urgency in his voice, and she quickly climbed the ladder, put on her deer hide shoes, and grabbed her leather pouch placing the strap over her head and across her body. Then she tossed their woven blankets to the floor below. When she got down the ladder, James handed Sarah her cape. Sarah noticed James's tomahawk was hanging by his side, and his sheathed knife was fastened across his chest.

"Put the medicine in your pouch," said James. Sarah did what he asked. Then she picked up the bag of food. James hurriedly wrote a note and placed it under a cup on the table:

> *Fort was burned. Mother and other settlers are missing. Fear the Indians have captured them. Heading west on Seneca Trail. Left April 29. Will bring Mother home soon. James and Sarah...and Duke*

Then James formed their blankets into rolls and tied leather straps around them. He slung one blanket over each of his shoulders. "I think we're ready now," he stated.

"What about Duke? Are we taking him?" inquired Sarah.

"I guess so. We can't just leave him penned in here, and if

we put him outside you know he'll follow us. We'll just have to put a rope on him so we can keep him close to us. Hopefully, he won't bark if we happen to see any Indians. I think he realizes something's wrong, too. Maybe he'll be able to help us find Mother." James grabbed a rope hanging from one of the pegs by the door. He opened the door and called for Duke who arrived quickly. James tied one end of the rope around Duke's neck, being careful not to get it too tight. Then they stepped outside and closed the door behind them.

James picked up his empty canteen. It was lying on the ground where he had tossed it the day before. They noticed there was no sign of the fish or the carrying sticks. Something, hopefully Duke instead of an old raccoon, must have dragged them away and had a nice feast. James took the lead, and the trio headed northwest toward the river. Although the sun was shining high in the sky, and the day was beautiful, their hearts were heavy. The determined looks on their faces revealed they were on an important mission. There was no time to stop and explore the plants, rocks, and insects they noticed along the way. Even Duke somehow knew this was a very different trip. He was rarely at the end of a rope. Soon they reached the river, and James filled their canteen.

"Take off your moccasins before you wade across, Sarah," instructed James who did the same.

After crossing the river, they once again donned their shoes. A few hundred feet up the hill they stepped onto an ancient trail. There were many paths through the forest made by animals, hunters, and trappers, but this path was almost as old as the mountains themselves. Father had told his children the Seneca Trail had been made centuries ago, probably by buffalo and elk coming down from the mountains heading for salt licks and grassy river bottoms. As they silently walked along, James thought of the numerous Indians who had also helped form this trail as they searched for that game.

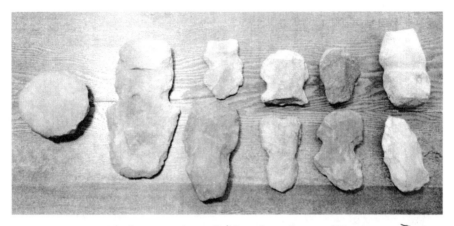

Native American field tools and stone lid

The Indians had also used this path to get to their crops near the river. He knew they had made clearings for their crops in the river bottoms. They did this by cutting off a ring of bark around the trees that grew there. This "girdling" killed the trees, causing the leaves to fall off. Then the light from the sun could get to the forest floor where the Indians planted what they called "The Three Sisters": corn, beans, and squash. Since the settlers had moved to the area, the Indians no longer used this path for hunting and planting purposes. Now, the Indians used this path to raid settlers on the frontier. That thought sent a chill up his spine!

Although James knew the settlers had learned much from the Indians' hunting and planting wisdom, he was very angry with them—angry that they had done this terrible thing. They had taken his Mother! He wished the settlers and the Indians could live together peaceably, but James knew the settlers had invaded this land the Indians claimed as theirs. The Indians were angry, too. James knew that was why they'd taken his mother and the others. He just hoped their anger wasn't too great!

CHAPTER 7

The gradual slope of the mountain trail soon turned into a steeper incline making walking more difficult. Duke wanted to bound after every rabbit and squirrel along the path, and James had to continually scold the dog and pull him back on the trail. James also kept an eye on his sister to make sure she stayed near him. Occasionally, he would quietly call to her to keep up with him, but he also slowed a little when he knew she needed rest.

When they reached the top of the first mountain, the going was easier for a short distance as the path leveled off. This allowed them to catch their breath. After a while, the path veered to the right. This part of the trail began fairly steep as it headed up the mountain, but thankfully, after a little while, it turned into a gradual incline.

Up and up they walked. James noticed the path had been following a small stream. At times they couldn't see the stream, but they would eventually end up near it farther along the trail. Finally, they reached the top of the second mountain and stopped for a few minutes to rest. Sarah was glad she could sit down. She opened the food pack and gave Duke and James each a Johnny cake, and she ate one, too. Then she handed James some of the dried berries and popped a few into her own mouth. She usually enjoyed the sweet, seedy huckleberries, but today they were flavorless. James handed Sarah the canteen, and after drinking the last of the water, she gave it back to him. He walked Duke over to the small stream and let him drink as he refilled the canteen. Then the two of them went back to where Sarah was resting. Neither of the children had spoken much up until this point, but now Sarah broke the silence, "James, how far do you think they've gone?"

"I don't know, but Father once said there are many mountains between us and the villages of the Delaware and Shawnee. We've only crossed two, so I'm sure we still have a long way to go. We need to get moving again. Are you rested enough?"

"I'm fine, James. Let's go find Mother," was Sarah's determined reply.

From the top of the mountain, the path headed down into a narrow gap. Travel was easier now that they didn't have to climb, but the trail was very rocky. The path was obvious, and James was hopeful they were headed in the right direction. Great cliffs towered on either side of them. Sarah noticed a beautiful red and yellow flower growing from crevices in the rocks. The ring of red spurs topping the blossoms resembled a circle of doves. She made a mental note to gather some of these for Mother on their way home. Sarah thought the flowers would look beautiful in the pitcher on the mantle and was sure her mother would love them. A tear slowly trickled from her eye.

It was now afternoon and the warm sun had gradually become hidden by thick, black clouds. Soon, a different scent in the air as well as a clap of thunder warned them that rain was nearby. Duke, who was not fond of stormy weather, now stayed near James.

"We need to find shelter soon," warned James.

Usually, in a rainstorm, a cedar tree was perfect shelter. Its thick evergreen branches would keep off much of the rain. Long ago, however, the children had learned that a tree was a dangerous place to seek shelter during a thunderstorm. James's eyes scanned the cliffs above the trail looking for an outcropping of rocks. He soon spotted what he thought would be the perfect place.

"Let's go up there, Sarah," he pointed. Sarah's eyes lifted to the cliff above them.

Sarah and Duke followed James as they scaled the steep bank. After stopping a few times to rest, they finally reached the outcropping. They crawled under the ledge and immediately noticed a small opening in the bank to the rear of it. Although they couldn't stand up under the ledge, they were able to sit comfortably.

Unfortunately, the rain had already started by the time they reached the shelter, and everyone was soaked. The wind was blowing, and now there was a definite chill in the air. James pulled Sarah's blanket off his back and handed it to her. She was shivering by the time she got it unrolled. She drew it around her shoulders, and although it was damp, it helped warm her. James unrolled his and threw it across his shoulders, too. Duke looked at Sarah and whined longingly. "Come on Duke," she called to him, and he crawled under her blanket, too.

"As soon as the rain lets up, I'll make a fire," James said to Sarah. It had crossed his mind that the Indians might see or smell the smoke and come after them, but he decided being up and away from the trail would help keep them safe. From the protection of the overhang, they could see the trail below.

James noticed the trees weren't leafed out as much up here as they were at home, so if anyone came by on the path, the children would be able to spot them quickly. James didn't think the Indians would back-track now anyway. They were most likely headed somewhere to the west.

When the rain slacked a bit, James placed his blanket across Sarah's shoulders and said, "I'll be back soon. I need to get some wood. Keep Duke here with you."

"I don't think Duke wants to go with you," said Sarah looking inside her blanket at the now sleeping mutt.

James stumbled over rocks through the light rain toward a pine tree on his right. Because of the tree's thickly-needled branches, the rain hadn't yet reached the ground underneath. The shed needles under its boughs were brown and dry. He gathered several handfuls and stuffed them in the pouch at his side. He also grabbed some small twigs lying about and used his tomahawk to cut off a few dead branches from the underside of the tree. He dragged the limbs to the outcropping where Sarah and Duke waited.

James got on his hands and knees and crawled under the ledge. Then he sat down, opened his small pouch, and pulled out the tin of fire-making materials. First, he formed the flax fibers into a nest putting a piece of char cloth in the hollow part. He then took out his flint and steel and held one in each hand just above the nest. He used the steel to strike the piece of flint causing tiny sparks to fall onto the char cloth. After several tries, the char cloth began to glow. James carefully picked up the flax and gently blew into it. Soon it started smoking, and then a flame erupted. When this happened he gently put the nest down and began adding the dry needles and small twigs. Once they caught fire, he used his tomahawk to chop small pieces of wood off the brittle pine branches. He then crisscrossed these on top of the burning twigs. They soon had a nice warm fire. Although some of the smoke occasionally drew back in on them, most of it funneled out along the edge of the rocks.

Making a fire using flint, steel, char cloth, and flax fibers

"Where'd you learn to do that?" asked Sarah as she handed James his blanket. She had been intently watching the whole process.

"Father taught me."

"I want to learn how to do it, too."

"I'll teach you when we get back home."

Tears filled Sarah's eyes again as she looked at James and asked, "When will that be?"

"I don't know Sarah, but we'll find Mother and get home as soon as we can."

"I do hope it's soon. I'm scared out here."

"I know, but Duke and I will take care of you. You're being very brave, and you're doing a good job keeping up with me."

"Thanks, James," Sarah said with a weak smile. "Sometimes I feel like complaining, but I bite my tongue."

"I know. I could complain, too, but it won't help anything," replied James. "Now, let's eat something. I think that'll help us both feel better."

Sarah roused Duke and forced him out from under her blanket. Then she picked up the food pouch beside her, untied the strip of leather, and took out a piece of deer jerky for him. "Here, Duke, you've been a good dog," she said as he wolfed the meat down. Next, she got a piece for herself and handed the bag to James. They sat by the fire eating quietly, each thinking private thoughts. The rain was pouring again, and thunder echoed through the gap and rumbled into the cave behind them. Duke whined and sat down against Sarah's leg. Finally James spoke, "It's probably best if we stay here tonight."

Sarah looked at her brother and nodded her approval. At least this place felt safer than out in the open, although the dark chasm behind them did make Sarah feel uncomfortable.

The rain had finally let up again, and James went out to collect more firewood. By the time he got back, the woods were getting dark. They were both thankful for the heat and light their small fire was emitting. Sarah watched as James picked up a short pine limb. She noticed one end of it was bulkier than the other. Her brother placed the large part in the flames, and soon the knot was burning brightly.

"I want to explore the cave, Sarah. You and Duke wait here."

"Are you sure, James?" Her eyes narrowed as she questioned his thinking. Sarah had been imagining wild animals, like those mean snakes with copper skin or wildcats, lurking in the dark cavern. Maybe even a polecat! Although she wasn't afraid of the black-and-white animals, she didn't want to get sprayed by one! She had been keeping one eye on the cave ever since they got there. She knew her brother could make sure there wasn't anything hiding in the darkness.

"OK," she finally said, "but Duke and I are going to move over to the other side of the ledge in case you chase out any wild creatures! And you'd better hurry back!" Her brother picked up the fiery limb, and Sarah grabbed a stick of wood, too—just in case. Then she and Duke moved out of harm's way.

Since the opening was too low for standing, James crawled into the dusky cave. The torch gave sufficient light to navigate as he wormed his way through the hole. Once inside, the ceiling was higher, and he was able to stand. He held the torch out in front of him and immediately saw the back wall about twelve feet ahead. The cave seemed to be about the size of their cabin. The damp air smelled musty as James peered around the dimly lit room. Shadows danced on the walls as the light shone around. Seeing no wild animals, he turned to leave.

Just then, his light flickered on a long form lying on his right where the cave's ceiling met the rocky wall. His breathing stopped as he shined his torch closer expecting to see a wildcat crouching there. Instead, his widened eyes focused on a man—an Indian lying there in the darkness. The man's eyes were closed, and he appeared to be asleep. James waited...frozen in place. He stood there a few long seconds watching for the

Indian's chest to expand. Nothing. No movement at all. The Indian was dead. Curiosity willed James forward. He had never been this close to an Indian, and he wanted a better look. The ceiling near the wall was lower, so he hunkered down as he slowly inched closer. James held his torch above the Indian's lifeless body. Focusing on the man's head, he saw it was wrapped in a blood-soaked bandage, and immediately James recalled the feathers and puddle of blood back at the fort. This must be the one, probably "buried" here by his companions, he reasoned.

Native American with gorget around his neck

Trade beads

James barely breathed as the flame revealed smudged black and red paint on the Indian's face. A string of blue beads, similar to his and Sarah's, and a silver crescent gorget lay on his dark, bare chest. A loincloth was attached at his waist and dirty bare feet showed below his buckskin leggings. James knew this Indian couldn't hurt him; nevertheless, he felt his insides begin to quiver. He had seen enough. He scrambled back toward the opening and quickly crawled out where Sarah waited. Once outside, he realized he had been holding his breath, and he sucked in a big gulp of air. Sarah immediately saw the terrified look on her brother's face and raised her stick. She expected to see a wild animal on James's heels. She scooted backwards, mindful of the ravine below her. Duke also jumped up, perked his ears, and woofed. "What's wrong, James?" Sarah quietly screamed.

"It's all right, Sarah! Don't panic! I was just in a hurry...to get back and tell you...there isn't anything in the cave...that can hurt us!" he stammered between breaths.

"You about scared us to death!" exclaimed Sarah as she lowered her stick. "Whew! We're safe, Duke!" she added as she hugged the dog's shoulders, calming them both.

"I'm sorry. I didn't mean to frighten you," said James as his heartbeat slowly returned to normal, and he settled beside the fire. "Everything's fine," he said out loud mostly to convince himself. "Now, let's get some sleep."

CHAPTER 8

James was startled awake the next morning. He thought he heard someone laughing. He opened his eyes and sat up abruptly nearly cracking his head against the roof of the ledge. There it was again! This time James recognized the sound. It was the call of a woodpecker. He could see its black and white feathers and red crest as it flitted up and down through the trees below them. James roused his sister, and she sat up, stretched as best as she could, and began rolling their blankets. Their fire had gone out sometime during the night, but James stirred it up as his father had taught him. Some coals still glowed under the ashes, and James poured water from the canteen on them. By that time, Sarah was ready to go, but before they crawled off the ledge, she reached into the food pouch and gave Duke a piece of jerky. He quickly gobbled down the food, and Sarah and James each took out a handful of nuts and berries. Within minutes the three of them were back on the trail.

James had been anxious to get away from the cave. While the sight of the dead Indian was unsettling, James was now even more confident their mother was somewhere ahead of them on this path. He really had no idea where he and Sarah were nor where they were headed. He just knew they had to stay on the trail. He'd never been on it before, except for crossing the section that passed near the settlement. It was forbidden for any of the youngsters to travel up the trail. Children were always warned they might be kidnapped by an Indian if they did. James had often yearned to explore the rutted path but knew if he had gotten caught doing that he would have been severely punished by his parents or maybe even captured by an Indian!

By midmorning they reached the mouth of the gap and walked into a wide green valley. From there, they could see layer upon layer of mountains rising in the west. For a brief moment, the children stood and stared in awe. Each range was higher than the one in front of it.

"Oh, James, these mountains go on forever!" whispered Sarah. James nodded and they continued on. As they traveled across the wide valley, both children silently worried that the trail might be endless. How far would they have to go to find their mother?

After walking about half an hour, James heard the sound of rushing water and immediately knew they were approaching a river. Since crossing the one near their home, the siblings hadn't come upon another river until now. The few small streams they had encountered up to this point could be crossed in one or two steps. As they drew nearer, James knew this river would be a bigger challenge since it was full from the snow melt and spring rains.

"What are we going to do now, James?" inquired Sarah as they stopped and gazed across the wide rushing water.

"We need to find a safe place to cross," answered James. As his eyes looked to the left, he noticed a mysterious black patch on a little knoll across the river. By now, Sarah had also seen it.

"What is that?" Sarah asked.

"I'm not sure, but we'll be able to see it better when we get to the other side."

"You take Duke and go that way," said James as he pointed north and handed Duke's rope to Sarah. "Look for a good place to cross the river."

James headed in the opposite direction. As he was scanning the area, his eyes fell across footprints in the sandy soil along the shore. He stooped and inspected them more closely. His father had taught him how to track animals in the forest, and he'd also paid close attention to the impression his own moccasins made in the ground. When he saw the prints, he instantly knew people had recently crossed here. James headed toward Sarah waving his arms. After he got her attention, he motioned for her to come toward him. When she was within hearing distance, James whispered loudly, "Look, Sarah! Footprints! Lots of 'em!" Sarah and Duke hurried to the spot where it was obvious others had made the crossing.

"The river is wide here, so it should be pretty shallow. I think we'll be able to walk all the way across without getting too wet." "Carry your moccasins," he advised her. The siblings took off their deer hide shoes and Sarah gave Duke's leash back to her brother. She gathered the bottom front of her dress together with one hand and held it up to her knees. She dropped her moccasins and the food pouch into the pocket made by her dress. Together, she and James stepped into the cold water. Sarah sucked in a breath of air as the frigid water crept higher on her legs. The river wasn't very deep, but in places Duke had to swim as his feet didn't quite touch the bottom. The smooth stones in the river were slippery and occasionally Sarah grabbed

James's arm with her free hand to steady herself. The children were used to balancing themselves on rocks—a game they enjoyed playing—hopping from rock to rock in the field behind their cabin. The loser was the first one whose foot touched the ground. However, rough field stones were definitely easier to stand on than these smooth river rocks.

Finally, they made it safely across the river and quickly put on their moccasins. Now they were close to the blackened spot they had noticed earlier, and it didn't take long to realize what it was—stockade poles. The sight reminded the children of the remains of their own fort. It took a few seconds for James's mind to register where they were.

"Oh no, James," whimpered Sarah. "Was that another fort?"

"I think it was Fort Upper Tract," he said hesitantly. "The Indians must have destroyed it too."

Fort Upper Tract monument

Arrowheads found in Upper Tract

"Do you think we should go up to it? Maybe we could find some settlers there."

"I don't think it's any use, Sarah. I'm sure the Indians didn't leave anyone there either. Besides, we need to keep moving."

"What if all the people in their settlement are gone, too? If they are, we might be the only ones left on the whole frontier," Sarah's voice quivered as she spoke.

"We're not alone, Sarah. Don't forget, Father and the other men will return soon. And we WILL find Mother and take her home with us!"

"I pray you are right, James."

"Come on, let's go." James quickly found the trail near the bank. Soon they were walking parallel to another stream which led them into a deep gap. James and Sarah were awed by the huge hemlock trees and vertical cliffs on either side of them. The layered, gray pillars looked as if they were sprouting from the earth. Bright green moss grew on some of the shaded rocks, giving them a softened texture.

The gap between the rocky cliffs narrowed as the trail snaked along the meandering stream. They walked on and on in silence. Sarah almost complained that she was tired but stopped before the words came out. She knew her brother was right. Complaints wouldn't help the situation. She knew she had to continue putting one foot in front of the other no matter how exhausted she was. She reminded herself that each step was a step closer to Mother.

Eventually, the gap began to widen, and they walked into a small clearing. Here the stream branched and the trail followed the smaller, right fork. As they rounded the bend, their eyes raised. An enormous mountain loomed ahead of them. It was much higher than any of the others they'd previously crossed. Sarah's voice broke the silence, "James, I hope we don't have to climb that one! I think each mountain is getter taller!"

"Maybe this path leads through a gap somewhere up there and we won't have to climb the steepest part of it," James commented. Nevertheless, they both quietly worried that the high mountain would be their next obstacle.

Suddenly, without warning, Duke's ears perked and his eyes looked toward the hill on their right. Sarah stopped in her tracks. "James," she whispered and he stopped, too, for by now, he had also heard something unfamiliar in the woods.

They both froze waiting for their heartbeats to slow so their hearing would be keener. There it was! They all heard it again. The children's widened eyes met, and their eyebrows raised questioning each other silently. This time, Duke bounded toward the sound causing James's arm to jerk violently as the rope pulled from his hand. "No, Duke," James said in a stern, but low voice. It was too late. Duke was charging up the steep bank with the rope trailing behind him. At that same moment, the eerie sound reached their ears again. No matter how much the children called to Duke, he ignored them. "Let's go, Sarah," ordered James. "We have to get him."

Sarah obeyed and followed closely behind her brother. She felt safer near him. They headed in the direction of the sound. Soon James realized the noise was coming from a dark spot against the side of the hill. Another cave. "The sound's coming from in there. Duke must have gone inside!" James whispered to Sarah as he pointed toward the cave's entrance.

James quietly climbed closer to the opening with Sarah on his heels. What had earlier sounded eerie now sounded mournful, like someone crying. James could only think it was another Indian waiting inside—only this one was alive! Suddenly the crying ceased, and what James and Sarah heard next stopped them in their tracks! Both children gasped as they recognized a sweet, familiar voice speaking to Duke.

At that moment, the dog bounded out the small opening. Mother was behind him crawling on her hands and knees. Her blond hair was tousled, and her face was streaked with tears. The homemade cape around her shoulders was muddy, and her dress was torn, but she had never looked more beautiful to them! The children immediately ran to her and fell to the ground beside her. Everyone began crying, laughing, and hugging at the same time. Even Duke joined in the celebration, barking as Mother vigorously rubbed his head and ears. James momentarily thought of Wallace, but didn't care what his friend would say about the tears streaming down his face.

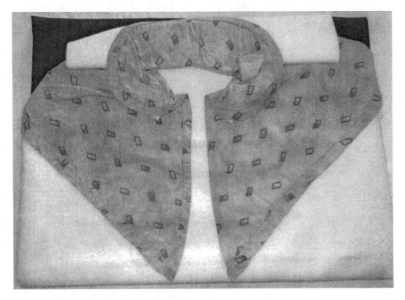

Sarah Dyer's cape

"Oh, Mother," sobbed Sarah. "We've been so worried about you!" Mother embraced Sarah, nearly squeezing the breath from her. Then Mother whispered, "I never stopped praying we would see each other again." Sarah's arms tightened around her Mother. She never wanted to let her go.

Mother's face turned toward James who was swiping his face with his sleeve. She hugged him tightly, too. "I'm so thankful you're both safe! I was afraid the Indians had hurt you!" she said through her flowing tears.

"We didn't see any Indians," replied Sarah. James said nothing.

"I'm glad...I wish I hadn't seen any of them either," said Mother sadly, as she gazed off into the distance. Then she looked at James and added, "How did you know where to find me?"

"After we read your letter, we went to the fort, but it was too late. I looked for our neighbors but couldn't find anyone, so I figured the Indians had captured everyone. At first, I wasn't positive they'd taken you on the Seneca Trail, but last night in the cave...I mean today when we found the footprints by the river, I knew we were headed in the right direction," explained James. Sarah didn't seem to notice her brother's slip-up.

"It was very dangerous for you to look for me!" added Mother firmly.

"But we had to find you! There wasn't anyone else who could help us! James wanted to leave me at home, but I was afraid to stay there. Please don't be angry, Mother!" pleaded Sarah through her tears.

"I'm not angry, child," said Mother pulling her daughter closer. "How could I be upset with you when I'm so grateful? You're both very brave!"

"What happened, Mother?" inquired James.

"We heard the alarm, and we went to the fort, but the Indians captured us there," said Mother.

"Our fort was burned to the ground," added James. "And so was Fort Upper Tract."

"I know, James," Mother sadly replied. Wanting to change the subject, she added, "We'll talk about all that later. I'm really thirsty and hungry. I do hope you've been drinking out of the streams like the deer, and there's some water left in that canteen!" she said with a wink. James smiled, reached to his side, and handed the canteen to his mother. She opened the top and took a long drink of the cool water. Then she pulled it away from her lips and said, "Thank you, James!" By now, Sarah had the food pack open and handed it to her Mother.

"Here, you can get what you want."

Mother looked into the sack. "Oh, children! What a feast!" She took out a large piece of jerky and some butternut kernels. She handed the bag back to Sarah who also took out some nuts. Then Sarah gave Duke a piece of jerky and offered the bag to James who grazed from it. James and Sarah watched as their mother devoured her food. They had never seen her eat so fast.

"Forgive my manners, children, but my stomach was gnawing my backbone!" Mother said as she finished her last bite of jerky. "Thank you! That was the best meal I've ever eaten!" After taking another drink from the canteen she announced, "Now I'm ready to go home, but you'll have to help me. My ankle is sprained and I won't be able to walk very fast."

James and Sarah looked down at Mother's swollen ankle atop her moccasin. It was misshapen and purple. "Wait, we brought something along that might help," said James. Sarah was already rummaging in her pouch. She handed the folded cloth to James, and he unwrapped the dried herbs. As soon as Mother saw them, she exclaimed, "Oh, children! How smart of you to bring these!"

"Well, I didn't know how long we'd have to search for you, and I wanted to be prepared for emergencies," replied James.

Mother looked her son. "Oh, James, your father will be so proud of you! *I'm* so proud of you! You've grown into a man right before our eyes!"

A wide smile crossed James's face. It spread from one ear to the other. Mother sat down and took off her moccasin. James pulled a sprig of sweet everlasting leaves from the packet and handed it to her. She stripped off the small narrow leaves and placed them in her palm.

"I know this water is supposed to be hot, but it's the best I can do right now," James said as he moistened the leaves with a little water from his canteen. Mother held the leaves until they had softened and then bruised them slightly. Next, she asked James for his knife and used it to cut a piece of material from the hem of her dress. James placed the leaves on the cloth and tightly wove it around his mother's ankle and across her foot several times. Then he tied the material in a knot on top of her foot to keep it in place. After Mother replaced her moccasin, the children stood up and carefully helped her to her feet.

"Wait," ordered James, as he walked to a nearby pine and chose a dead limb from the ground under it. He used his hatchet to cut off the protruding twigs around the limb and walked back to his mother. He handed the makeshift cane to her.

"Thank you, James," she said as she used the walking stick to keep herself steady. "I think I can make it now! Let's go home," she added with a smile.

James tied Duke's rope around his belt. Then James and Sarah got on either side of Mother. They carefully led her down the side of the ridge and back onto the path. Everyone was relieved to finally be heading east instead of west. Travel was slower this time with their mother hobbling along, but she assured James that his cane was perfect and the poultice was helping with the pain.

CHAPTER 9

By noon, they approached the remains of Fort Upper Tract again. As they passed it, Mother wiped tears from her eyes and uttered a prayer for the settlers of the area. This time the river crossing proved to be extra tricky, but after a few slips they made it safely across without getting completely soaked. At least the sun was warm, and it didn't take long for their clothes to dry as they traveled along. By late evening, they had made it to the gap where the children had spent the previous night. As they headed up the rocky hollow, the sun slipped below the mountains behind them and the forest began to darken.

"We need to stop and rest for the night," said Mother grimacing. "My foot is really hurting again." She and Sarah found some large rocks where they could sit comfortably while James and Duke scouted for a suitable sleeping place. Soon, James found a mossy patch to the right of the trail. It was hidden behind a stand of very large hemlocks, and James felt it would be a safe place to spend the night. He went back to get his mother and Sarah.

"I found a good place to rest," he announced as he helped his mother to her feet. When they reached the spot, Sarah spread their blankets on the ground, and they all sat down. Mother took the cloth off her ankle. "Oh, it feels so good to be sitting!" she declared as she rubbed her foot. James asked Sarah for more of the sweet everlasting leaves, and when Mother was ready, he rewrapped her ankle. Then Sarah opened the food pack, took out her portion of jerky as well as a piece for Duke, and passed it to the others. As they ate, Sarah spoke up, "Mother, tell us what happened back at the fort."

"There's so much to tell," Mother sighed and began. "About an hour after you went fishing, Nicholas rode by on his horse yelling, *Fort up!* I knew there were Indians in the area. As soon as I heard his alarm, I ran to the river looking for you, but I couldn't find you. I was so upset. I convinced myself that you had heard the alarm too and had already gone to the fort. I couldn't yell for you for fear the Indians were already nearby and would hear me. I was afraid if they found me, they might find you, too. After a brief pause, Mother questioned, "Where were you two?"

"We fished north instead of south," replied James sheepishly. "I knew about a great fishing spot down river, so we went there. I'm sorry Mother. I should have told you where we were going." Mother's eyes widened, and she nodded.

"Well," she continued, "when I couldn't find you, I hurried back home and wrote a note for you to meet me at the fort."

"We didn't make it back home until later in the afternoon. We found your note and ran to the fort," replied James, "but there wasn't anybody there, and the fort had burned to the ground."

"We'd already been forced to begin walking on the trail," added Mother. "The Indians set fire to the fort as we left."

"I looked, but couldn't find any evidence to show that anyone had even been at the fort," replied James.

"We *were* there—about forty of us. We hadn't been inside long when we heard several shots close by. Suddenly, the fort was surrounded by a band of Indians. There was a Frenchman with them, too. I heard him call the Indian, who appeared to be the chief, Killbuck. Killbuck could speak English, and Captain Seybert spoke with him through the wall of the fort.

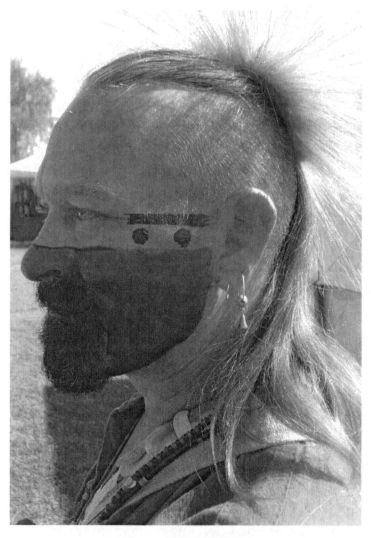

Senecan descendant

Men dressed in French-style clothing standing
in front of a wikiup (Shawnee hut)

Following their conversation, Captain Seybert spoke with us and told us we would have to surrender because we didn't have enough men or ammunition to defend ourselves. He said the Indians promised to treat us kindly if we surrendered. We trusted the captain, but as the gate was swinging open, we heard a shot come from the blockhouse above us. Someone later told me Nicholas had tried to shoot Killbuck. Supposedly

Captain Seybert grabbed Nicholas's arm as he shot, so he missed his mark.

After that, everything was in chaos. The Indians ran into the fort and began grabbing everyone. They pulled us outside. Women were screaming; children were crying. I did see Mr. Robertson get away through the brush along the bank. As far as I know, they never caught him. The Indians got everyone out of the fort, except Mrs. Hannah Hinkle. God rest her soul. She was too weak to walk so they left her there.

"But Mother," interrupted James, "When I looked around, I didn't see anyone!"

"I'm sure she was in there," Mother replied.

James recalled the pile of burned logs from the blockhouse. "She must have been buried in the rubble," he said sadly.

"I'm thankful you didn't see her—or any of the others who were left behind," added Mother. "I'm sure God spared you from that sight." Mother closed her eyes as a tear trickled down her cheek. She wiped it away and continued.

"The Indians then gathered up everything they could: guns, tomahawks, anything they thought would be valuable or useful. They even filled a kettle with the smaller items like bowls and utensils...and our *Bible*. I'd taken it to the fort with me. Two of the Indians came out carrying the kettle on a pole between them. I saw the *Bible* on top of the other things. I'm not sure why they wanted it. Maybe somehow they sensed how special it is."

"Once they got out with the kettle, the fort was set on fire. Then we had to walk up the hill west of the fort where the Indians separated us into two groups. The older, feeble ones were forced to sit down on a log." Tears now began streaming down Mother's face as she recalled the terrible scene that had unfolded before her.

"Mother you don't have to tell us anymore," said Sarah quietly.

Mother took a deep breath and composed herself. Then she sadly replied. "I'll just say only the younger, healthier group, including a baby, was spared. After the massacre, there were probably about twenty of us left. We were numb with grief as we were forced to begin walking on the trail. Killbuck and a few Indians walked in front of us, the settlers were next in line, and more Indians and the kettle-bearers behind us. One Indian had been shot in the head back at the fort. He was being carried on a litter by two other Indians. They brought up the rear.

After about an hour of walking, I heard the baby start crying. The Indians seemed agitated. I guess they thought the baby was making too much noise, but...he didn't cry for long. He's with the angels now." Mother choked on her words, and again, her eyes welled up with tears. She shook her head to clear her mind as she continued.

"Somewhere along the path, before we stopped for the night, the Indians who were carrying the kettle came up missing. They didn't join up with us until later. I don't know what they did with the kettle, but when they came back, they didn't have it anymore. They must have gotten tired of carrying it. I'm sure it was very heavy. Just the kettle by itself would have been hard to carry up the mountain—even for two people. I was saddened to think our *Bible* was probably gone forever but thankful I've stored many passages from it in my heart. Those verses gave me the strength and courage to continue on."

We walked until evening. After the sun set, we stopped and spent the night up in this gap. The injured Indian must have died along the way because when we stopped for the night, he was carried to a cave up on the steep mountainside," she pointed up the trail. "They left him there."

"This is the gap we stayed in last night Mother!" exclaimed Sarah. "We stayed on a high ledge, and there was a cave behind us. James crawled in and looked around, but there wasn't anything in it. I sure am glad it wasn't the same cave with the dead Indian inside!" James kept a straight face and made no comment as he looked toward the steep hillside.

Sarah was anxious to know more so it wasn't long before she asked, "How did you escape, Mother?"

"Well, I knew if I didn't think of something I might never see my family again. That gave me the courage to do what I did. I realized each day would take me farther away from you and your father, so I knew I had to get away somehow. The next morning, after we crossed the river, I was near the front of the group but gradually allowed myself to be overtaken by all but two warriors who were bringing up the rear. I knew my only hope was to get off the path and hide."

"My mind raced trying to think of a way to escape. We had just reached the area where you found me when all at once, a deer darted across the path directly in front of me. The two warriors walking behind me sprinted after it. As soon as they took off after the deer, I dropped over the stream bank on the opposite side of the trail and disappeared in the thick laurel. I lay down and pulled dried leaves over me. I tried to stay silent, but my heart wouldn't listen to me. I'm sure if someone had walked near me they could have heard it beating, but thankfully no one ever came back."

"I don't know how long it took before they realized I was

gone, but by the time they did, they'd probably gone too far to send anyone back to search for me. When I finally thought it was safe, I came out of my hiding place. I knew I shouldn't get back on the trail, so instead I crossed it and headed up the steep hill on the other side. I was hoping to follow the trail home from above. Then the unthinkable happened. A loose rock rolled under my foot, and I sprained my ankle. As I was stumbling along, I saw the opening in the side of the hill and crawled inside to spend the night. Sitting there in the darkness during the storm, I prayed that God would help me, and He answered my prayer! He sent you to find me!"

"I was praying, too, Mother," said James.

"So was I," added Sarah.

Mother hugged both children tightly. Sarah's mind still lingered on the missing kettle her mother had mentioned. "So is the kettle still out here somewhere?" she asked as she looked around curiously.

"I'm sure it is. It's probably on the other side of the mountain up there. I don't think they got this far with it. It would have been too difficult to carry it down through these rocks. I don't remember where we were when I noticed the braves had left the trail with it, but I'm sure they never went back to get it," replied Mother.

"Maybe we can find it and return everything that was taken," said Sarah.

"Well, I'm afraid most of the people who owned those things are...gone," she said sadly.

"What about the men who weren't at the settlement?" asked Sarah. "I know they will want their things back."

"What they'll want…is their loved ones…and I'm afraid for most of them that isn't going to happen," said Mother softly.

"Why did the Indians do such a horrible thing?" inquired Sarah.

"I'm sure one reason is because the Indians are very angry with us for settling on their hunting lands," answered Mother.

"Who did they kill, Mother? Are Nicholas and Wallace still alive?" asked James.

"Nicholas was taken captive, and as far as I know, he's still with the Indians. Sadly, Wallace was killed. I'm so sorry, James."

James turned his head. He was thankful Nicholas was alive but shocked to hear his friend and mentor was gone. In Wallace's honor, he forced himself not to cry. Wallace would have been proud of him. It was the one last thing he could do for his special friend.

"I don't want to talk anymore," stated Mother. "We need to get some rest now. We still have a long way to go, and it'll take us a while to get home," she said looking down at her still-swollen ankle.

Although they were fairly confident the Indians wouldn't backtrack, James thought it would be best if they didn't light a fire. It wasn't as chilly as it had been the night before, and thankfully, it wasn't raining. Mother lay on her back and pulled the children closer to her—one on either side—and quietly whispered, "I love you both and am grateful to God you are safe."

"We love you, too," said James as Sarah wiggled closer to her mother. James had tied Duke's rope to a nearby sapling, and he lay at their feet. They were comforted by the fact that the dog's keen ears would be on guard throughout the night. Everyone was exhausted and quickly fell asleep. They slept soundly, knowing Duke would alert them of any danger.

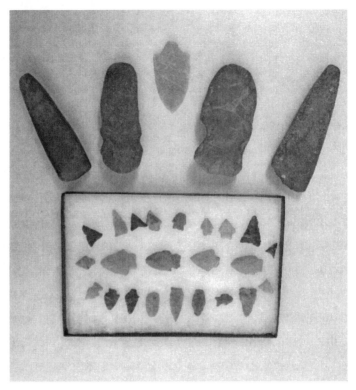

Artifacts found at Fort Seybert

CHAPTER 10

Mother was used to waking early, and at the crack of dawn when her eyes opened, she woke the children. They were all anxious to get home. Sarah doled out breakfast. Their supply of food was dwindling, but still Sarah made sure Duke had his equal share since being on a tether prevented him from hunting for himself. Of course, they still had the hard tack, but because no one liked the tasteless squares, it would be saved until last.

James renewed the poultice on Mother's ankle, and they headed up the rocky path. She used her cane and hobbled as best as she could. The remedy was helping, but her ankle was still very stiff and sore. The children took turns aiding Mother, and holding Duke's rope.

Sarah was taking a turn walking with Mother when suddenly, her brother, who was in the lead, stopped the procession. "Shh, someone's coming up ahead," he announced. "Quick, hide!" Duke's ears perked and his tail began wagging." James kept a good hold on the dog's rope as they all scrambled to the side of the trail and hid behind some large, round boulders.

"What if it's Indians?" whispered Sarah.

"I don't think it's Indians," quietly replied James. "Look at Duke." Sarah and Mother noticed the excitement in Duke's tail. "And Indians probably wouldn't be coming from the east anyway. But, we have to be careful just in case!"

All at once, through the branches ahead, Sarah saw a familiar brown, felt hat with a turkey feather protruding from it. "It's Father!" she exclaimed. Mother burst into tears as the children and Duke ran to meet him. Along with Father were ten other men from the settlement, including Mr. Robertson and one man they had never seen before. When Father saw the children, he jumped from his horse, ran to them, and hugged them tightly. Then he hesitantly asked, "Did you find your mother?"

"Down there," Sarah pointed toward the huge rocks just as Mother appeared from behind one of them. Father rushed to her. When he reached her, his arms wrapped tightly around her as she sobbed.

"I thought I had lost all of you," Father said through his own tears. The children hurried to them and joined in the hug. For a while, no one could speak. Duke whined excitedly and ran circles around the family twining his rope around their legs.

By now, the other men had joined the Dyers, and Father introduced his family to Captain Brock, the leader of the search party. Mother wiped her eyes with her cape as she spoke to the men and quickly recounted her story for them. Captain Brock informed Mother that some of the men had stayed behind at the settlement to bury their loved ones. The massacred settlers were being placed in a common grave on the hillside where they had been found. The searchers were in a hurry to continue on, so after a quick good-bye, Captain Brock and the other men headed west. They were hopeful they could rescue the remaining captives.

Common grave site at Fort Seybert

Plaque on wall at grave site

After the search party left, the Dyer family continued their reunion. "I was afraid I would never see any of you again!" Father's voice quivered as he spoke.

"I'm so glad James and Sarah came to find me," explained Mother. "I would never have been able to make it this far on my own."

"Don't forget Duke," added Sarah, "He's the one who knew you were in that cave."

Father reached down and petted the mutt on his head. Then Father looked at James. "I'm proud of you, young man. I knew you wouldn't let me down. I'm proud of you, too, Sarah," he said as he pulled his daughter close to him. Then Father walked to his horse and took two items from his pack. First he handed a gift to James. "Every man needs a new tomahawk," he told his son.

James proudly took the tomahawk. He turned it over and over in his hands. "Thank you, Father!" he exclaimed. "How did you know I wanted this?" James asked with a twinkle in his eye. Father smiled and shrugged.

Next Father presented Sarah her gift. She carefully took the small carved replica of a ship from his hand. "I know you have some wanderlust in your heart, Sarah, as I did at your age. I hope one day you can travel across the ocean and meet your far-away family."

Sarah hugged him tightly. "Oh, Father, I love it!" she exclaimed. Mother was holding Duke's leash, and next, Father looked down at him.

"Well, ole Duke, if I would have known what a hero you are, I would have brought you a gift too!"

"I'm taking care of Duke's reward. I'm breaking my own

rule!" Mother exclaimed with a smile. "From now on, Duke will stay in the house with us!"

"Did you hear that, Duke?" asked James. "You're not just a dog anymore; now you're part of our family!" James patted his own chest and Duke put his paws up against him. James rubbed the dog's ears lovingly.

"It's time to go home," said Father. He gently picked up the children's mother, carried her to his horse, and carefully placed her in the saddle.

"Wait!" shouted Sarah. "We need to celebrate!" She opened the food sack and took out the four small cakes of sugar. She knew Duke was not a lover of sweets, so she tossed him the last piece of jerky. Then she presented the sugar cakes to her family. James quickly shoved the treat into his mouth.

"Oh, Sarah, this is just perfect!" exclaimed Mother.

"I'd rather have some hard tack, Sarah!" joked Father.

"OK," replied Sarah as she rummaged in the food pack. "I have some right here."

"No, no, that's all right," Father quickly replied as he positioned the cake in his jaw, then added, "By the way, it's May first. Why are you children still wearing your moccasins? That's costing me shoe leather!" Everyone chuckled as Sarah popped the last sugar cake into her mouth.

The family headed single-file toward home. Father was in front leading his horse where Mother rode comfortably. Next, Duke walked in front of James. Sarah brought up the rear, the sugar cake slowly melting in her mouth releasing its delightful maple flavor. She was amazed at how much easier this trip seemed now that they were heading home. She scanned the area as they walked along the trail, hopeful she would catch a glimpse of the abandoned kettle somewhere among the massive trees and stones. If she found it, she knew she could help get everything back to normal. Sarah desperately wanted to return the items to their rightful owners. She especially wanted to find their family *Bible*.

Many times she was sure she spotted the kettle. Her eyes would be drawn to something in the distance that looked promising. As they approached the object, however, it would turn out to be a big boulder or a rotten stump.

Finally, as the sun set in the west, Sarah's family topped the last summit of their journey. They stood side-by-side and their eyes scanned the South Fork Valley. A mixture of emotions filled their hearts: relief, sorrow, and happiness. They knew their lives would never be the same, but they were together. Right now that was all that mattered.

Sarah put her hands behind her back as she walked near her mother. "Welcome home, Mother," she said as she pulled her hands around and produced the slightly wilted bouquet of red and yellow flowers she had secretly picked earlier. Mother smiled through her tears as she reached for the columbines. "They're beautiful, Sarah. Thank you!" Father took Sarah's hand and put his other arm across James's shoulder. "We're home," he said.

James's eyes looked across the valley. At that moment, he realized that even though many of the settlers were gone, his father would never move from this place. Father was like the apple trees he had planted years ago—firmly rooted in the ground. James understood his father's love for this land because he loved it, too.

Once again Father took the lead as the family headed down

the slope toward their cabin. Sarah walked a few steps, but then stopped to take a long, thoughtful look behind her. As she peered into the darkening forest, she recalled what had been hidden there: Mother, the other captives, the dead Indian, the kettle. Thankfully, Mother had been found. Sarah thought of the search party and hoped they would find the rest of the captive settlers and be back home soon, too. Maybe one day, someone traveling along the trail would even discover the cave where the bones of the deceased Indian were concealed—but what about the kettle?

Sarah visualized the large, black kettle filled with cherished possessions. *Will anyone ever find it?* she wondered. While she considered this question, it was answered deep in her heart. Somehow she knew it would never be found. The kettle would remain hidden in the mountains surrounded by enormous trees, moss-covered boulders, and dark caves.

Sarah turned and resumed her descent into the valley. Her bright blue eyes now focused on her family ahead of her, and she smiled. "That kettle might be gone forever, but I'm thankful I still have the most precious treasure of all," Sarah whispered aloud as she hurried down the path toward it.

MORE INFORMATION ABOUT THE PHOTOS IN THIS BOOK

Chapter 1:

– Author's drawing showing the carvings on the back of Sarah Dyer Hawes' blackened, buffalo horn spoon. Sarah brought the spoon home with her when she returned from the Shawnee village where she was held captive for 3 ½ years. A photo of the spoon can be seen on page 17 in *A History of Pendleton County, West Virginia* by Oren F. Morton.

– This rustic cabin is owned by Jed Conrad and sits near the site of Fort Seybert. Early settlers like the Dyers would have lived in similar structures, but roofs during that time period would have been covered with long, thin slabs of logs or wooden shingles.

Chapter 2:

– Pothcrbs (leafy vegetables and herbs used for seasoning food) and medicinal herbs were planted along the outside walls of the cabins with woven twig fences surrounding the plants to keep out livestock. The large, fuzzy-leafed plant on the right is mullein. Also note the honey bee skep to the back of the garden. Picture taken at Prickett's Fort, a Revolutionary War era replica, near Fairmont, WV.

- Frontiersmen made many pieces of their clothing from buckskin. Buckskin would have held up better than cloth. Jed Conrad made most of the things he is wearing in this photograph.
- Pelts of animals were taken to a trading post where they were traded for needed items. Picture taken at Prickett's Fort.
- Items including powder horns would have been used as trade goods.

Chapter 3:

- Tomahawks displayed at Fort Seybert during the Treasure Mountain Festival.

Chapter 4:

- Photos of a replica of Fort Seybert going up in flames at the reenactment during the 2014 Treasure Mountain Festival. Each year a new model of the fort is built and burned.

Chapter 5:

- -Picture of table taken at Prickett's Fort.

Chapter 6:

- Spinning wheels were used to spin wool into yarn or flax into linen thread. This picture was taken at Prickett's Fort.
- Sarah Dyer Hawes Davis and her husband Robert Davis had this blanket chest made for their daughter, Rachel. It is constructed of walnut and has the year 1794 and a six-pointed diamond star carved on the front. It was probably crafted in the Shenandoah Valley. It is now owned by John Dalen.
- John Dalen also owns this dark brown, stoneware pitcher which belonged to Roger Dyer of the Dyer Settlement. Roger was Sarah and James's father and was born in 1705 and died in 1758. John Dalen is an eighth generation descendant of Roger Dyer.
- These Native American field tools and stone lid were found in Hardy County, West Virginia, which borders Pendleton County. The former home of the Dyer family was in Old Fields, also in Hardy County.

Chapter 7:

- Dave Snyder demonstrates how to make fire using flint (left hand), steel (right hand), a small bundle of flax fibers, and char cloth. The tin can with the two holes in the lid is used when making the char cloth.
- Greg Cougevan of New York portrays a Mohawk, an ally of the French and Shawnee, during the Treasure Mountain Festival at Fort Seybert. The silver, crescent-shaped

gorget /gor'-jet/ around his neck was made by Robert Croukshank, a famous Scottish-born silversmith who lived from 1748 to 1809. French and British officers wore gorgets to show their rank. Native Americans would take gorgets from slain British officers, and sometimes the French gave gorgets to the native people for their help in battle. It would have been a great honor to wear a gorget, and those who possessed them would be respected by others in their tribe.

- These are authentic, blue, glass trade beads made in Czechoslovakia. Beads like these would have been given to the Native Americans by the Dutch, English, or French in exchange for furs. Owner: Greg Cougevan.

Chapter 8:

- This monument is in Upper Tract on the Morris Mallow farm. It sits in a beautiful spot overlooking the South Branch of the Potomac River and the valley surrounding it. Morris's father, Olin Mallow, helped build the monument. The following information is engraved on the plaque:

Fort Upper Tract

Site of a 60 x 60 foot stockade with blockhouse in center. One of a chain of forts authorized by the Virginia Assembly in 1756 to protect settlers in the South Branch Valley. Erected and garrisoned under orders of Colonel George Washington. Captured by the Indians and burned April 27, 1758. Captain James Dunlap and 21 others massacred. None known to have escaped.

The massacred:

Captain James Dunlap, Josiah Wilson, John Hutcheson, Thomas Caddon, Henry McCullom, John Wright, Thomas Smith, Robert McNulty, William Elliott and wife, Adam Little, Ludwig Falck and wife, _____ Brock, John Ramsey, William Burk, _____ Rooney, William Woods, John McCulley, Thomas Searl, James Gill, John Gay.

Erected by Pendleton County Historical Society and South Branch Ruitans. Dedicated Sept. 17, 1971.

- Arrowheads found on the Morris Mallow farm near the site of Fort Upper Tract. The various shapes indicate the time period in which they were used. This proves Native Americans were in this area for thousands of years. A good reference for determining the age of arrowheads is www.projectilepoints.net.
- This cape belonged to Sarah Dyer and is now owned by Patricia Boggs Alt, a seventh generation descendant of Sarah. It is on display at the Boggs House Museum in Franklin, WV.

Chapter 9:

- Corey Taylor from the state of New York, a descendant of the Senecan Nation, portrays an ally of the French and Shawnee during the Treasure Mountain Festival at Fort Seybert.

- George Kinnison (left) and Jack Hasselaar (right) portray Frenchmen at Fort Seybert. George is wearing a French-style waistcoat, and Jack has on a Voyager hat. They are both wearing leggings. George is holding a French-made, flint-lock musket called a "Fusil". This reliable, light-weight gun was good for hunting and was popular during the French and Indian War period (1754-1763). Behind them is a wikiup, a thatched, cattail-leaf hut. The Shawnee would have stayed in structures like this. Sometimes the frame of the hut, which was made of bent willow saplings, would have been covered with elm bark shingles instead of cattail leaves, depending on the materials in the area.
- All of these artifacts were found at Fort Seybert and span thousands of years. The spearhead (top center) was found a few hundred yards west of the gravesite of the massacred settlers. The two large stones (top left and right) are called "celts" /selts/ and were probably used when working with wood. The other two stones (top) are ax heads. Some of the arrowheads in the case are made from flint, quartz, and red jasper. The black ones (very dark) could have been made from flint, also called chert, found in Pendleton County.

Chapter 10:

- Grave site of settlers who were massacred at Fort Seybert. The rock wall surrounding the common grave was built

in the 1930's by The Roger Dyer Family Association. Note the white oak trees near the wall. According to an old photograph, these trees were already large when the wall was built. White oaks only grow 12-14 inches per year and can reach a height of 150 feet. They can live 200-300 years (some as much as 450 years). Could these trees have been planted when the settlers were buried?
— Plaque on rock wall at grave site.

Additional photos and information:

In 1756, the leaders of Virginia (Virginia General Assembly) voted to build 23 forts along the frontier to protect the settlers. Two of these forts were Fort Upper Tract (near Hugh Mann's Mill), and Trout Rock Fort. The fort at Trout Rock supposedly stood near Route 220 about four miles south of Franklin, but it is possible that this fort was never built. Colonel George Washington was the Commander in Chief of the forces who built and manned these forts. There were six known forts built in Pendleton County between 1750 and 1764. The other four forts in Pendleton County at that time were built for protection by families who moved into the area: Hinkle Fort in Germany Valley, Fort Skidmore at Ruddle, Fort Seybert (later Blizzard's Fort), and one fort with an unknown name. None of the forts remain.

This sign at Fort Seybert states that there was a three-day siege, although the fort may have been overtaken in one day.

This is believed to be the site of the original Fort Seybert. Efforts are being made to build a permanent replica here. Some of the blockhouse logs have been stacked to dry. Shenandoah Mountain stands in the distance.

Site of Trout Rock Fort

Site of Fort Skidmore

(The house in the background is not part of the fort.)

Site of Hinkle Fort

This model of a fort was constructed in the late 1970's by the author's dad, Jesse Short. He built it for the author's brother, Kelly. This fort has the blockhouse built in one corner and living quarters built along the inside walls of the stockade (some forts were built in this fashion). Fort Seybert looked different: It supposedly had a circular stockade (fence) with a diameter of 30 yards. A two-story, twenty-foot-square blockhouse stood in the center where settlers would have lived when they were confined at the fort.

Pendleton County, WV Settlement Timeline

For thousands of years, evidence shows that Native Americans occupied the river bottoms of Pendleton County, West Virginia (then Virginia).

Later, the Shawnee utilized the valleys of Pendleton. They did not believe in actual ownership of land, but the valleys were used for hunting. The wild animals in the area, as well as the Native American hunters, made footpaths that went from one valley to another. One of these paths led from Moorefield to Elkins, passing through the Seneca Rocks area. Another route went from Seneca Rocks to Fort Seybert. Residents of Pendleton County call these paths the Seneca Trail. These paths were actually branches of the main Seneca Trail, or Great Indian War and Trading Path which ran from New York to Alabama.

1745: Abraham Burner was the first settler in Pendleton County, living about half a mile below Brandywine.

1746-47: Robert Green of Culpeper, Virginia surveyed land in Pendleton County, including 2,643 acres at Fort Seybert.

1747: Six families bought 1,860 acres in the Fort Seybert area for $203.33. The families were: Roger Dyer and his son, William, his son-in-law Matthew Patton, John Patton, Jr., John Smith, and William Stephenson.

1753: Many immigrants settled in the area. For a period of time, the Native Americans and settlers were "friendly" with each other. Some of the Shawnee learned the English language from the fur trappers and settlers, and the two groups shared ideas on food preparation and medicine.

1754-1763: French and Indian War. Both the French and British wanted to own the Ohio Valley area. The Native Americans and French traded goods and were "friends," but the Native Americans didn't get along with the British because these settlers built cabins and established settlements on their hunting grounds. As a result, the Native Americans, including the Delaware and Shawnee, helped the French attack British frontier settlements.

1756: To make settlers feel safer, a line of forts and blockhouses was built by the British along the eastern edge of the Allegheny Mountains in Virginia (part of which is now West Virginia). Virginia used $33,333 to build 23 forts. The forts were built about 15 miles apart. George Washington ordered Captain Waggoner and 60 men to build two forts in the upper South Branch area. These were Trout Rock Fort and Fort Upper Tract.

1757: Before this date, there is no evidence of any Indian raids into what is now Pendleton County.

April 27, 1758: Medicine man and chief of the Delaware warriors, "Bemino", also known as John Killbuck, Sr., led an attack on Fort Upper Tract. Shawnee warriors and probably some Frenchmen joined the Delawares. They killed approximately 27 settlers. It is thought that none of the settlers survived as there are no written accounts of the attack.

April 28, 1758: The same group who attacked Fort Upper Tract attacked Fort Seybert.

1760: French lost power in America.

1764: There were no further raids into what is now Pendleton County. The Native Americans had to release 32 men and 58 women and children from their villages in Ohio. These settlers went back to their homes in Virginia (and West Virginia). Some settlers had to be taken away from the Native Americans by force because they had grown up with them and did not want to leave.

1788: Pendleton County was formed from parts of Augusta and Rockingham Counties (Virginia) and Hardy County (then Virginia, now West Virginia).

June 20, 1863: West Virginia became a state.

Timeline of Events at Fort Seybert

1755: Mr. Patton sold land to Jacob Seybert, and a fort was built on that land near what was called the Dyer Settlement. There were several families living in this area, including the Dyers.

Thursday, April 27, 1758: Most of the able-bodied men and a few women and children from the Fort Seybert area headed east across the Shenandoah Mountain to trade their winter furs for supplies.

Friday, April 28, 1758 (There are differing accounts of the following events.): It was a foggy morning. Peter Hawes' wife and an indentured servant boy named Wallace were going to shear sheep or milk a cow. A Native American appeared and the woman tried to stab him with sheep shears, but the two settlers were captured.

William Dyer, one of Sarah Dyer Hawes' brothers, was supposedly out hunting. He was shot and killed.

Forty to fifty settlers "fort up." It is possible the settlers had moved into the fort (for safety) the day before, when the others left for the Shenandoah Valley.

Approximately forty Shawnee and Delaware warriors and at least one Frenchman, led by Delaware war chief Killbuck, attacked Fort Seybert. Killbuck may have led this attack and the one at Fort Upper Tract because he was angry over an incident that had happened between him and Peter Casey who lived in Old Fields.

Nicholas Seybert wounded a Native American. Nicholas also attempted to shoot Killbuck, but someone (possibly his father, Jacob) in the fort prevented this by pushing his arm aside as he shot.

Captain Jacob Seybert ordered the fort's gate be opened after Killbuck promised not to hurt the settlers. However, when the gate was opened the settlers were captured.

Possibly 6-8 women and children and a man named Mr. Robertson escaped. Mr. Robertson went across Shenandoah Mountain to get help.

The settlers were taken outside and the fort set on fire. A bedfast woman, Hannah Hinkle, died in the fire.

The captives were taken approximately a quarter mile up the hillside and separated into two groups. One group was tomahawked and left for dead. A total of at least 17 were killed, including Captain Jacob Seybert and his wife, a Wallace boy, Henry Haus, and John Regger and his wife. Also killed were James and Sarah's father, Roger Dyer; their brother, William Dyer; and probably their mother, Hannah Smith Dyer.

There may have been as many as 24 taken captive. The known group of settlers who was taken captive included: Mrs. Michael (Mary) Mallo and her five children (they may have been captured later in Greenawalt Gap), Mrs. Jacob Peterson, a Hevener girl, Hannah (no known last name) and a baby who was killed along the trail (possibly Mary Mallo's). Also captured were James Dyer, who was fourteen at the time, and his eighteen-year-old sister, Sarah Dyer Hawes.

Following the raid on Fort Seybert, the Native Americans and their captives traveled west on the Seneca Trail. This trail possibly went from Fort Seybert, across Siple Mountain and then through Deep Hollow. From there, they traveled into Greenawalt Gap, five miles away from Fort Seybert, where they spent the first night. The Native American who had been injured at the fort died along the trail and was left in a shallow cave or outcropping in Greenawalt Gap. Supposedly his skeleton could be seen there for many years.

Saturday, April 29, 1758: The journey continued through Kline, Upper Tract, up Reed's Creek Road, and then onto Pretty Ridge Road. The modern-day roads between Fort Seybert and Pretty Ridge Road partially follow this part of the ancient trail.

About one mile up Pretty Ridge Road, the group would have gone through what is now the property of Stanley and Ruth Kile, my husband's parents. Then they would have crossed North Mountain at a low place along the rocky ridge locals call "The Creep," and headed into Germany Valley. Once in the valley, they would have probably headed through Roy Gap. Their next stop was Seneca Rocks. They would have covered approximately 16 miles on this second day of their journey. A Harper girl related to Philip Harper and a girl from Grant County were captured at Seneca Rocks.

Sunday, April 30, 1758: The Native Americans and their captives headed from Seneca Rocks toward Elkins, following another branch of the Seneca Trail that is sometimes called the Shawnee Trail (because the Shawnee warriors traveled this part of the trail when raiding settlements).

(From this point, there is no written account of how long the journey took): From Elkins they went on to Chillecothe, Ohio, where the captives were distributed among Delaware and Shawnee villages in the area. This would have been approximately 300 miles on foot!

A legend has been passed down for centuries that tells of a kettle full of "treasures" which was also taken from Fort Seybert. The French and Native Americans would have plundered anything of value from the fort. Two Native Americans carried the kettle on a pole between them, but abandoned it somewhere along the trail. It is believed the kettle was never retrieved as the Native Americans supposedly never returned to the area.

Mr. Robertson, who had escaped from the fort, made it to the Shenandoah Valley, and a search party under the command of Captain Brock came to help but was too late. They buried the victims on the hill where they died. They were buried in one, large grave west of the site of the fort.

George Washington estimated 60 people at Fort Upper Tract and Fort Seybert were killed. Some of the remaining people temporarily left the area. However, for a while, some of the settlers in the Fort Seybert area may have stayed in caves along the Shenandoah Mountain for safety. From there, they could have gone down into the South Fork Valley to tend their crops, taking watch dogs with them.

Fort Seybert was supposedly rebuilt and renamed Blizzard's Fort after the new owner of the property.

To commemorate these events, the Treasure Mountain Festival is held each year on the third weekend of September in Fort Seybert and Franklin, West Virginia. A reenactment of the massacre, including the burning of the fort is portrayed at Fort Seybert.

Visit this site to find out more about the Treasure Mountain Festival: http://tmf.squarespace.com/the-fort-burning/

An added note

It is believed the Dyers were either of British or Scotch-Irish descent; possibly from an area near the border between Scotland and England. James Dyer was born in 1744 in Pennsylvania and died in 1807. He was captured at the age of 14 and lived with the Indians for two years before escaping and returning to Pendleton County. He is buried at Fort Seybert. His sister, Sarah Dyer Hawes was born in 1740 and died in 1816, and is buried in Brandywine, WV. She was taken by the Indians at age 18 and was a captive for three and a half years until James was able to help free her. Henry Hawes, her first husband had died before Sarah was captured. She married Robert Davis after she returned to Pendleton County.

While gathering information for this book, I learned that my husband is an eighth generation descendant of Michael and Mary Mallo (now spelled "Mallow" in Pendleton County). Mary and her five children (six including Henry who was born in November of 1758) were captured by Killbuck's group. Mary's husband, Michael, was away from home at the time. Mrs. Mallo and three of her children returned to Pendleton County years later. One of her young daughters had been killed, but it is not known what happened to the other two children. When Mary came home, it was reported that she spoke of the kettle of "treasure" that had been abandoned by the warriors somewhere along the trail.

"Shawnee Cakes, Johnny Cakes, Janiken, Journey Cakes, or Fried Mush"

All of the above are names for basically the same food. The Native Americans grew corn, and after it was harvested, they dried and shelled it. Sometimes, the kernels of corn were placed in a hollowed out piece of wood. A wooden mallet was then used to grind the kernels into cornmeal. The corn could also be ground between two rocks. Water was added to the cornmeal and the mixture was formed into little cakes. Native Americans baked these cakes on rocks near their campfires.

The Shawnee taught the early settlers how to grow corn and make these cakes. Therefore, the settlers called the cakes "Shawnee cakes." However, since the settlers had iron skillets, they sometimes fried their cakes in some sort of animal fat instead of baking them.

This food has also been called "Johnny cake" maybe because "Shawnee" sounds like "Johnny." "Janiken" is the Native American word for "corn cake," and when settlers traveled they took these cakes along and called them "journey cakes." Some people in Pendleton County call this food "fried mush," although mush is a little different because this cornmeal and water mixture is cooked and poured into a greased loaf pan to cool. It is then sliced and the slabs are fried in a skillet.

The Native Americans and settlers also made maple syrup and gathered honey which at times were used to sweeten the baked or fried cakes.

Another name for this food could be "Delicious!" Try some!

Recipe for Johnny Cakes
(Adult supervision is required)

Ingredients: 1 cup corn meal, about 1 ½ cups boiling water, a pinch of salt

Directions: In a mixing bowl, combine the corn meal and salt. Then carefully stir in the boiling water to make a very thick batter. Use a serving spoon to put spoonfuls of mixture into a skillet of hot lard or oil. Use a second spoon to scrape the batter off the first spoon as you make the cakes. Then use the back of one of the spoons to flatten the cakes a little. The batter may stick to the spoon when you do this, so dip the back of the spoon in skillet oil before pressing onto cakes. Brown cakes on both sides. Eat warm with maple syrup or honey on top. Yum! Yum!

For your consideration:

1. Mother didn't know where to find the children when the alarm sounded. Explain why. How could this problem have been avoided?
2. Knowing life on the frontier could be dangerous, infer why people moved there anyway.
3. What evidence suggests Sarah was afraid as she and James fished? Support your answer with details from the text.
4. Identify some of the lessons the children had learned that are still important for us today.
5. Analyze why James kept some "little details" to himself instead of sharing them with Sarah.
6. Evaluate James's decision to search for his mother. Explain why you think he made the right or wrong decision?
7. Visualize Fort Seybert or the interior of the Dyer cabin and choose one to illustrate.
8. Research the introduction of honey bees and apple trees to North America. Describe how these natural resources benefit our country's economy.
9. Did the mountains really get higher as the children headed west on the trail? Explain.
10. In your opinion, why do you think there are differing versions of the events at Fort Seybert on April 28, 1758? Why isn't there much evidence about what happened at Fort Upper Tract?
11. Compare/Contrast the "Fort Seybert Events Timeline" with the fictional novel. How are they alike/different?

12. Make a prediction about how the events at Fort Seybert on April 28, 1758 may have been different if most of the men had been at the fort instead of in the Shenandoah Valley during the attack.
13. On the second map in this book, trace the path the captive settlers were forced to follow. Draw a conclusion about where you think the kettle of "treasure" was abandoned.
14. List some natural "treasures" that CAN be found in the Appalachian Mountains of West Virginia.
15. Interview family members and write a summary of your own history.

To read interesting articles about West Virginia—past and present—visit www.wvencyclopedia.org

BIBLIOGRAPHY

Adamson, Greg. "Killbuck." *e-WV: The West Virginia Encyclopedia*. 03 December 2015.Web.14 July 2016.

Adamson, Greg. "Fort Upper Tract." *e-WV: The West Virginia Encyclopedia*. 07 February 2012. Web. 07 September 2016.

Adamson, Greg. "Fort Seybert." *e-WV: The West Virginia Encyclopedia*. Web. 14 July 2016.

Boggs, Elsie Byrd. *The Hammers and Allied Families of Pendleton County, West Virginia*. Parsons, WV: McClain Printing Company, 1989. Print

Carvell, Kenneth. "Sylvan Grassy Glades Boon to Early Settlers." *WV Magazine*: June 1981, Vol. 45, no. 4: p. 20. Print.

DeHass, Wills. *History of the Early Settlement and Indian Wars of Western Virginia: Embracing an Account of Various Expeditions in the West, Previous to 1795; Also Biographical Sketches*. Wheeling: H. Hoblitell, 1851. Print.

Fast, Richard Ellsworth, and Hu Maxwell. *The History and Government of West Virginia*: The Acme Publishing Company

1901. https://archive.org/details/historyandgover01maxwgoog Web. 5 April 2016.

Foster, Steven and Duke, James, *The Peterson Field Guide Series: A Field Guide to Medicinal Plants and Herbs of Eastern and Central North America.* Boston: Houghton Mifflin Company, 2000. Print.

Harman, Pauline Ruddle. *Ruddle-Riddle Genealogy and Biography.* Salem, WV: Walsworth Publishing, 1984. Print.

Larrivee, Andrea Dalen. "A Variety of Accounts of the Indian Raids on Fort Upper Tract and Fort Seybert." Family Ties, Fort Seybert. http://family.ties.tripod.com/fort_seybert.htm Web. 6 Sept. 2016.

Maxwell, Hu and Thomas Condit Miller. *West Virginia and its People:* Lewis Historical Publishing Company, 1913. https://archive.org/details/westvirginiaitsp02mill Web. 7 July 2016.

McBride, Kim and Stephen McBride "Frontier Defense." *e-WV: The West Virginia Encyclopedia.* 23 April 2013. Web. 06 May 2015.

McBride, W. Stephen, Ph.D., Kim Arbogast McBride, Ph.D., and Greg Adamson, M.S. *Frontier Forts in West Virginia, Historical and Archaeological Exploration.* Charleston: West Virginia Division of Culture and History, 2003. Print.

McWhorter, JC. *The Border Settlers of Northwestern Virginia from 1768 to 1795 Embracing the Life of Jesse Hughes and*

Other Noted Scouts of the Trans-Allegheny, with notes and illustrative anecdotes by Lucullus Virgil McWhorter. Hamilton, OH: The Republican Publishing Company, 1915. Print.

Morton, Oren F. *A History of Pendleton County West Virginia*. Harrisonburg, Virginia: C.J. Carrier Company, 2001, Print.

"Quercus alba" Wikipedia, the free encyclopedia. https://en.wikipedia.org/wiki/Quercus_alba Web. 22 September 2016.

Rice, Donald L. "The Seneca Trail." *e-WV: The West Virginia Encyclopedia*. 29 October 2010. Web. 06 September 2016.

Stradley, Linda. "Johnnycakes." Whatscookingamerica.net/History/Johnnycakes.htm. 2004 Web. 19 July 2016.

Summers, George W. "Fort Seybert Massacre." West Virginia Division of Culture and History, *Charleston Daily Mail*. 01 Jan. 1939. http://www.wvculture.org/history/settlement/fortseybert03.html Web. 18 Sept. 2013.

Talbot, Mary Lee Keister. *The Dyer Settlement, The Fort Seybert Massacre*. Dingle Print Co., 1937. http://www.usgennet.org/usa/ga/topic/indian/coldyer.htm Web. 2 Feb. 2016.

Talbot, Mrs. Lee Keister, "New Interpretations of Fort Seybert, Fort Seybert Massacre." West Virginia Division of Culture and History, *Grant County Press*. 13 May 1937, http://www.wvculture.org/history/settlement/fortseybert01.html Web. 7 April 2016.

Thompson, Robert. *A Woman of Courage on the West Virginia Frontier: Phebe Tucker Cunningham*. Charleston, SC: The History Press, 2013. Print.

Tillson 1, Albert H. "The Southern Backcountry: A Survey of Current Research." *The Virginia Magazine of History and Biography*. Vol.98 No. 3, 1990. http://www.jstor.org/stable/4249162 Web. 14 July 2016.

Withers, Alexander Scott. *Chronicles of Border Warfare:* Stewart and Kidd, 1895. http://www.wvculture.org/hiStory/settlement/fortseybert02.html Web. 12 Sept. 2014.

CPSIA information can be obtained
at www.ICGtesting.com
Printed in the USA
LVOW08s1128020717

540115LV00002B/277/P